Tomorrowing

Tomorrowing

Terry Bisson

DUKE UNIVERSITY PRESS
Durham and London
2024

© 2024 TERRY BISSON
Printed in the United States of America on acid-free paper ∞
Project Editor: Lisa Lawley
Designed by A. Mattson Gallagher
Typeset in Untitled Serif and General Sans
by Copperline Book Services

Library of Congress Cataloging-in-Publication Data
Names: Bisson, Terry, author.
Title: Tomorrowing / Terry Bisson.
Other titles: Practices.
Description: Durham : Duke University Press, 2024. | Series: Practices
Identifiers: LCCN 2023042683 (print)
LCCN 2023042684 (ebook)
ISBN 9781478030683 (paperback)
ISBN 9781478026457 (hardcover)
ISBN 9781478059660 (ebook)
Subjects: BISAC: FICTION / Science Fiction / General | LCGFT:
Fiction. | Science fiction.
Classification: LCC PS3552.I7736 T66 2024 (print) |
LCC PS3552.I7736 (ebook) | DDC 813/.54—dc23/eng/20240220
LC record available at https://lccn.loc.gov/2023042683
LC ebook record available at https://lccn.loc.gov/2023042684

Cover text handwritten by Terry Bisson.

publication supported by a grant from
The Community Foundation for Greater New Haven
as part of the **Urban Haven Project**

My thanks to
Kim Stanley Robinson,
Locus,
and Judy . . . "Still the One"

CONTENTS

April 1, 2004. Locus magazine, the Variety *of the science fiction and fantasy field, publishes its first This Month in History
feature, thus beginning, with little notice or fanfare, what is
destined to become the longest-running trade magazine fiction
feature in the universe.*

True story, not an April fool.

The idea came to me from a newspaper; I forget which one.
I had been a working science fiction writer for some twenty
years in New York, and newspapers are fodder for SF story
ideas. For fun I always checked out the Today or This Day in
History features: those with events everyone remembers —
wars, disasters, elections, assassinations, and so forth.

One day, I forget which one, the idea came to me: Why not
move the history to the future? It seemed an easy idea for any
SF writer, a group who often regard the future as their native

land, or at least their hometown. And I was surprised that no one had thought of it before. A small but interesting idea, and I could play it for humor, for horror, for SF spec, for maybe all together.

Meanwhile, my wife, Judy, and I were planning to move to California, so I pitched the idea to Eileen Gunn, a writer and editor who had just started Infinite Matrix, an SF website financed with Silicon Valley money. Eileen could pay top dollar, so she cast for the big names—Ursula Le Guin, Bill Gibson, Lucius Shepard, Bruce Sterling, &c—and I was eager to be included in such company.

"Sure," Eileen said. "Could be fun. Have at it."

So I did up a few items for her, I forget which ones, and they appeared on Infinite Matrix as This Week in History. But appearing once per day, without the monthly framing device, my few lines didn't get much notice. They looked lost. Plus, Eileen's website was livelier and more varied than any SF magazine (my usual markets) could be, and her big names included underground comix greats like Gilbert Shelton and Paul Mavrides of *The Fabulous Furry Freak Brothers*. Overwhelmed and outperformed, I moved on to bigger projects (some with Eileen) and let my original idea slip away.

Meanwhile, Judy and I moved to California and found a house in Oakland.

There I got to know *Locus* and Charles Brown. They were sort of the same thing. Charles was already a legend in the tiny but close-knit world of SF. He was not a writer but a serious reader—an intelligent, worldly, cultured SF fan who knew and kept up with the field and all the writers. His *Locus* in the early 1970s was originally an 8 × 11 fanzine focusing on SF and "published" as a stapled, xeroxed giveaway. Under Charles, *Locus* survived and flourished. By the time I moved to the Bay Area in 2002, *Locus* was a slick four-color monthly, flush with SF publishers' ads and filled with reviews, interviews, award news, convention pics, and industry gossip about agents, authors, editors, and fans. Everything about SF but SF itself. It was now the official trade magazine of the SF and fantasy publishing field. Still is.

It was published out of Charles's house in Oakland Hills. Charles was the William Shawn of *Locus*, the moody wizard in chief, but the magazine itself was put together every month by a very capable, by now professional, handpicked team of sharp young SF enthusiasts, mostly attractive women (a weakness Charles treasured) and a few guys and some interns. I had of course met Charles at SF cons, but only for a handshake with the old guy who knew everybody and who everybody knew. Now I was a local writer, a neighbor, and I was always welcome to drop by. And often did.

I liked the whole *Locus* crew, but Charles and I hit it off big-time. A certifiable eccentric who sometimes padded around the "office" barefoot, he was often gruff and demanding (especially of his staff) but always confidently brilliant—even scholarly and clever—with a shrewd understanding of genre literature and what it could, and shouldn't, do. A largely self-educated navy vet, he loved SF for the literary life it had given him, and he made *Locus* a home for every type—the high and the low. I often hung out with him after his younger staff had split for the day. Charles was old and fat and slow (and knew it), but I was pushing sixty myself, and he liked that. He liked my work, and I liked that. He was from Brooklyn, and he liked that I was also a nostalgic New Yorker of a different but familiar sort—the small-town kid who seeks the city and stays. He took me to the San Francisco Symphony, for which he had season tickets and needed a friend to drive and park his car. I was part of the *Locus* circle at the cons around the United States—and even in China once, for SF is international and Charles always needed a luggage wrangler. There were parties, too, and I got to know his famous friends and adversaries, for he hung closely to both. Tight with money and parsimonious with praise, Charles was generous with Scotch (always single malt) and high-end wine.

I think he also liked the fact that, already established in the field, I wasn't trying to get something out of him. One night we were musing about the role of luck in literature, the perils of freelancing, or some such, and I remembered my This Week in History that hadn't quite worked on Eileen's Infinite Matrix website, which was already part of SF history. Charles shrugged, I seem to remember, and said, "*Locus* needs a monthly. We could give it a shot. I can give you fifty bucks."

I hadn't pitched it, but he had caught it. And as usual he was right. I think I shrugged OK. Then he got fresh glasses and poured us both another shot of Scotch. Every variety of single malt, according to Charles, requires a differently shaped snifter. That night was Highland Park, from Orkney.

There was never a word from Charles or *Locus* about what This Month in History should be. It was entirely up to me. I decided I could handle four short items a month, and the items soon developed a tone. One of the *Locus* staff, Amelia Beamer, described it as a "satire or parody of journalese," and I realized, *Of course!* I was keeping it attached to its newspaper roots. Fiction as fact.

So that was the first rule, and it still holds. Every item started with an event. Often (not always) led with a headline. The results of that event reported rather than explained, and rather dryly as well.

The rest of the process emerged from SF itself, but easily, as the feature embodies my tendencies in SF. The items were all separate, unrelated, each with a different novelty or surprise or insight. There was usually an item about outer space or other planets, in keeping with SF's origins as a promotional literature for space travel. No goblins or wizards or magic rings, please. The tomorrows are usually only a century or two away, in keeping with Kim Stanley Robinson's understanding that SF is mostly about the present. I tried to mix a little good news with the bad, as I found the dystopian tone of today's SF tiresome.

Oh, and shorter was better. I got less wordy as the months and years rolled by. Getting with the process was easy for me, for I made it up as I went along. Charles never said anything about it, which was his way, which I took as approval.

In 2009, when Charles Brown died, as we all must do, he did it in his own way: peacefully, flying home in business class from Readercon in New England with a pretty woman from his staff by his side. He fell asleep and never woke up—an unforgettable, accomplished, and lucky man.

He left *Locus* and the house to "the girls" as he (still, sometimes) called them, though they had long outgrown his more antediluvian notions. The *Locus* staff was already diversified and capable, and the magazine has flourished under their manly as well as womanly hands. The formidably talented Liza Trombi took the helm and even gave me a raise. I sometimes wryly refer to This Month in History as my day job, as if anyone could live on eighty bucks a month. But in its own way, it is.

That's the end of this story, twenty years ago; but it begins some sixty years before.

I had never intended to be a science fiction writer. True, SF was my first literature as a teen in the 1950s—the golden age of Ray Bradbury, Arthur C. Clarke, Clifford Simak, Isaac Asimov. Paperbacks with rocket-ship covers in drugstore racks, in a town without bookstores, taught me what literature could do: stir the imagination, even the soul. By the 1960s I had moved on to Ernest Hemingway, F. Scott Fitzgerald, J. D. Salinger—more serious stuff. The Beat Generation lit me up like a roman candle, particularly Jack Kerouac's epic Byronic needfulness. Big boy stuff.

I knew only one sure thing: I wanted to be a writer. So I wrote a Kerouacian clone and (surprise!) interested a literary agent and split for the city. In another era (another bildungsroman) it would have been London or Paris, but for me, for small-town America, it was New York City, of course.

And, of course, the novel never sold. Novels rarely do, and first novels hardly ever. My agent strolled away. But there I was, in the beating heart of the publishing world! I wrote for romance, astrology, and Western magazines and supermarket tabloids ("Sasquatch Marries California Teen"); I took on paperback cover copy, even book catalogs and comics and kids' books. It was hack work, but I was a writer, wasn't I? It was mostly fun, and I was learning the ropes, wasn't I?

Meanwhile, I devoted my mornings to my next, my new, my real, my soon-to-be-celebrated novel. It had to be perfect, of course, and the longer I worked on it, the shorter it got. Revising my revisions was miserable work. I dreaded those mornings.

Then I got lucky.

I was writing cover copy for David Hartwell, the editor of a paperback fantasy and SF series—some old, some new. One day he sat me down and said, "Your high fantasy copy has the right tone, the syntax and the sound." (He meant pompous faux-biblical.) "Why not write the book as well?" Huh? "Give me a two-page plot outline, and I can advance you fifteen hundred dollars."

Write a novel for money? "No, no, no," I said. For all the right reasons. I was a serious wannabe mainstream novelist, no hack, and I held out resolutely for several weeks before I caved and went to work. I made $1,600 and learned that you don't have to write a masterpiece. You just have to make up a story and spin it out well. A serious lesson and a liberating one.

Hartwell published my first book (to slim success) and sat me down again. "Now write the book you want to write," he said. So I did. I put in it everything I knew about the South, small towns, girls and cars and guns, and made up the rest. And guess what? It was SF! It was fantasy! All in a weird mix, which meant that it was no bestseller but got read by the right people. It got noticed.

David Hartwell, one of the now-legendary creators of modern SF, was my editor for the next several decades. I soon knew all the SF editors, most of the writers, and many of the fans. He had plunged me into the world that I wanted (without knowing it) and that now wanted me (at least a little). It was then a small and welcoming world, with writers both very good and just good enough. And I had made the team!

Science fiction is an often-overlooked, sometimes-scorned genre in which the play of ideas is often the action; an outlier of literature, even dismissed as less than art: rock 'n' roll, not a symphony. (Some of us like that.) But I was at home there and still am. That's why Hartwell and Charles Brown are the proper bookends for this book. David pulled me into SF, and Charles gave me my longest assignment. Which is still my day job.

But enough about me. And This Month in History can speak for itself. I describe it on my website (easy to find) as "the longest-running trade magazine fiction feature in the Universe," which, I suppose, in fact, it is.

And here, finally (firstly?), it is. In full.

This Month in History

Locus, April 2004 – July 2023

2004

APRIL 1, 2044. Green House occupied. After months of delays, President George F. Parks and "First Guy" Carlo Moon move in, with their dogs, praising the moveable walls, solar panels and grass roof of the eco structure that replaces the former White House, now the Clinton Wax Museum.

APRIL 19, 3144. Life found on tiny Centauran planetoid. An apparent one-time event ends in tragedy as a 4-centimeter-wide slime mold on S2000-J1 is discovered, photographed, tagged, catalogued, and immediately dies.

APRIL 24, 2102. Art vandal pardoned. Alma Farnsley, the woman who destroyed all the works of art in the Louvre, the Met and the Prado before she was stopped by an alert security guard, is released from prison at age 74. Farnsley returns to her home on the Isle of Woman, where she will be elected governor for six consecutive terms.

APRIL 7, 2265. Lunar Chardonnay wins Double Gold at San Francisco International Wine Competition. This is the first major award for the sprawling Burroughs Vineyard, a joint project of Coppola Ltd. and NASA Inc. The winning entry is described as "a hearty but subtle white, chilly on first encounter, but with a lingering finish as forgiving as moonlight."

MAY 7, 2011. Martha Stewart released. President Clinton signs a controversial pardon for the celebrated entrepreneur, who has been held in solitary confinement and denied cutlery since the "mess hall melee," which resulted in the disfigurement of cellmate Donna Karan. The president declines comment, noting only that Stewart is "no longer a threat to public safety."

MAY 14, 3602. Sparkle Plenty dies at age 1,182 (est.), thus ending the millennia-long life of the world's favorite (and indeed, only) resident extraterrestrial. The affectionate arthropod never revealed where she came from or why, but the mystery only added to her immense popularity, especially with children.

MAY 19, 2009. Amtrak offloaded to India. The fourth derailment in three months (and the 256th in two decades) prompts Congress to cut the price for a quick sale. "If Amtrak were an airline, it would have been shut down years ago," says Speaker Kennedy, who opposed the sale on humanitarian grounds.

MAY 26, 2117. Library of Congress wiped out. The entire e-collection is erased by a single "suicide book" written by a disgruntled science fiction author. The unsuspecting employee who downloaded the deadly volume (*Last Planet Down*) is treated and released by volunteer grief counselors.

JUNE 6, 2044. The USA is officially declared a trilingual country by President Ramirez. In a Rose Garden ceremony the first opera-star president sings "God Bless America" in Bengali, English and Spanish, alternating verses.

JUNE 9, 3104. St. Louis des Étoiles falls. Centuries of slow orbital decay end in "a blaze of glory" witnessed by millions as the faithful, the respectful and the curious turn out to bid farewell to the planet's first orbiting cathedral.

JUNE 16, 2113. Enhanced redwood downed. Ecoterrorists in California topple the world's tallest tree, the 1,325-meter General Ashcroft. The genetically enhanced giant, which was over a century old, demolishes a cheese plant, a regional airport and an assisted living facility when it falls.

JUNE 25, 2012. Muscle car protest. Forty-three thousand SUVs jam Washington's fabled beltway to protest the Nader Tax, establishing a $1 monthly "atmosphere use fee" for every cubic centimeter of engine displacement over 1,500 cc. With the passage of the law in January, President Nader's approval rating fell from 24% to a term low of .66%.

JULY 5, 2044. Heads of state of 21 nations and 53 NGOs turn out for funeral of Earth's last elephant. The great beast was electrocuted by an illegal power tap in suburban Lagos, where it had apparently retreated from the brush fires raging through central Africa. It was previously thought that the last elephant had been killed in 2036, when the "Dumbo virus" raged through the world's zoos.

JULY 11, 2189. Renewed fighting in Los Angeles between the Earl of Water and the Count of Electricity. Disorder spreads to freeways as gangs of "underpass boys" take 8 and 5, setting fire to stalled cars.

JULY 22, 2033. Seg does AT. Bill Wright, who lost a leg in a snow-boarding accident, reaches the summit of Maine's 1,605-meter Katahdin, becoming the first Segway HT rider to complete the 3,500-kilometer Appalachian Trail. Wright's epic three-month journey, which included a gun battle in a Pennsylvania mall and an erotic encounter with a genetically modified mink, is later chronicled in his e-bestseller *Two Wheels, One Dream*.

JULY 36, 4377. Heaven's Gate (also known as Hale-Bopp) is viewed up close by millions via atmospheric lensing as the comet makes its first sojourn to the inner solar system since 1997. Nike pseudofoot sales soar.

AUGUST 9, 2722. Box sells for .5 million. A 20th-century card-board box, described by Sotheby-Christie CEO Alma Grohn as "an exquisite example of a humble art," sells at auction for a record W4,935,984. The half-meter-square container for Cheerios, a late-modern mood-enhancer, was allegedly found in the ruins of a former "film" star's mansion on Beverly Island, Cafonia.

AUGUST 14, 2049. Hung jury in Ballantine triple-murder trial. Phone calls result in a statistical dead heat, prompting Judge Lance Ito III to declare a mistrial and pundits to question the new system in which criminal defendants are tried in the media and voted on by the public.

AUGUST 21, 2206. Big Mac dies. The celebrated 1,456-square-mile, 125-meter-high proti-beeve expires of septicemia. The tragedy is discovered by cowboys riding line on a hormone drip when their ATV falls into an unhealed lesion. Four western Nebraska counties evacuated.

AUGUST 29, 2109. TrumpNation stuck. The world's first fully free-floating artificial principality, seeking refuge in the Mediterranean after a stormy summer in the English Channel, runs aground on a shoal in the Strait of Gibraltar. Both Israel and the Islamic Republic of Spain claim salvage rights.

SEPTEMBER 4, 2011. Reparations Day celebrated nationwide as Harvard, Yale, Brown and Dartmouth turn over their endowments to the trustees of the United Negro College Fund. The undisclosed sum, estimated in the tens of billions, was revealed to be the profits (with interest) of the slave trade.

SEPTEMBER 8, 2203. Sargasso Station goes online. It is hoped that the massive nuclear-powered pumping facility will restart the Gulf Stream and lead to the eventual resettlement of Europe.

SEPTEMBER 19, 2723. Saturn station massacre. Tragedy strikes Colomere Orbital Music Camp in the rings of Saturn when a jealous husband opens fire on the interim conductor (his wife), then kills half the audience and himself with a mail-order morbidity compressor. The massacre and subsequent attempts to rescue the survivors are later immortalized in Orlo-Pienne's classic opera, *Embrodud a Ringolée*.

SEPTEMBER 23, 2046. Hydrogen bomb levels Grand Canyon. A thermonuclear device floated down the Colorado River smooths the canyon walls, killing 1,200 and obliterating nature's handiwork of 11 million years. EarthLast's Willis Avenue Unit claims responsibility, in protest of environmental restrictions on Antarctic melt-and-drill technology.

OCTOBER 9, 2017. President Obama signs "Ella Bill," promising new housing and jobs for refugees from the deadliest of the stationary weather systems which have plagued North America and central Asia. Ella, which settled over the lower Ohio Valley in the spring of 2014, features continuous rainfall and winds of 75 to 85 mph.

OCTOBER 13, 2406. Eiffel Tower reopens. The historically authentic ferrous structure contains four sections of the original, which was destroyed and scattered by glacial ice.

OCTOBER 20, 2116. Orbiting cemetery looted. Hollywood's prestigious Starlawn Memorial Sky Garden is closed for renovations after an unexpected meteor shower delights viewers across the Midwest and a charred 10-millimeter section of Leonardo DiCaprio's pelvis sells on eBay for €210,000.

OCTOBER 22, 2028. Viagra Seat banned. After months of investigation, prompted by an article in *Spokes* magazine, the World Sports Authority votes 445–12 to ban the device, which diverts chemically enhanced blood flow to the upper thighs. Four bicycle racers, led by the aging Lance Armstrong, begin a hunger strike in protest.

NOVEMBER 7, 2322. Oldest bio-building burns. A five-alarm fire destroys the historic Prairie Manor apartment complex in Decatur, Illinois. Grown from seed by AgriBild, a division of Pfister-DuPont, the 22nd-century apartment complex was designated a National Landmark in 2307. The fire, which claims three lives, is blamed on corn borers, which ate a section of a heating flue.

NOVEMBER 13, 2097. Walt Disney dies again. The reanimated DNA holorep, who used his celebrity/curiosity status to gain control of the legendary entertainment empire, dies of organ attrition at re-age 34, unmourned after laying off hundreds of thousands and declaring the biggest bankruptcy since Enron in 2001.

NOVEMBER 22, 2019. Terror victim tells all. A tearful Tawana Brawley finally tells the whole story of her 1987 kidnapping and rape to a secret Homeland Security court. The unidentified assailants are given indeterminate sentences after being convicted of undisclosed crimes in a closed 90-minute trial. As he was sealing the records, Attorney General Sharpton expressed his satisfaction but noted that "justice delayed is justice denied."

NOVEMBER 29, 2406. *Krishna Sovereign* crashes on Mars. The illegal squatter ship, the first to enter Mars's volatile new atmosphere since the Red Planet was diverted into Earth orbit in 2399, is swept away by flash flooding in Chasma Cobert—1,254 die.

DECEMBER 2, 2032. Free speech camp opens. President Cheney staples a ceremonial barbed-wire strand to officially open Camp Kunstler in Nevada's Ashcroft Desert. The 1,244 guests, who are allowed a complete range of expression during their mandatory six-week stay, are each given a bullhorn on arrival but must buy their own batteries.

DECEMBER 11, 2165. Christmas concert cancelled. The annual Lincoln Center benefit by untrained musicians with nano-enhanced hands is called off when a solar flare renders the participants unable to play the opening chords of *The Nutcracker*

Suite. Volunteers from the audience help the orchestra members tie their shoelaces and pack their instruments for the bus trip back to Pennsylvania.

DECEMBER 19, 2066. Capote great-grandson hosts formal blast. The hundredth anniversary of Truman Capote's famous party at the Plaza Hotel is commemorated by his "cheerfully illegitimate" descendant, Beauregard, at Staten Island's historic Plaza Motel. Among the hundreds attending are four New Jersey mayors, a gay fire chief and a movie star. All wear black tie.

DECEMBER 22, 2015. Lunar "face" wiped out. The crater Nonius, which for centuries has appeared as Padre Pio to some and as Satan to others, is obliterated by suicide astronauts in a stolen Soyuz rocket. Islamic Correction claims responsibility.

2005

JANUARY 2, 2023. Film opening breaks billion mark. *The Return of the Mummy's Daughter Returns Again 2* shatters holiday box office records with a $1.2 billion opening on 323,456 screens worldwide. The previous record of $.9 billion was held by the 2018 Winfrey-Tarantino feely *Daddy? No!*

JANUARY 9, 2063. Last prison in US closes. Attica, once the scene of a historic rebellion, is to be turned into a museum to commemorate the sufferings caused for centuries by the incarceratory penal system, now replaced by corporal and chemical sanctions.

JANUARY 16, 2153. Elvis coin pulled. The $10 gold piece commemorating the 20th-century rock star is removed from circulation by the Vegas Mint after complaints from local merchants that it was too easy to counterfeit.

JANUARY 29, 2481. Hudson Bay freezes over. Celebrants from around the world, many dressed in white in memory of the extinct polar bear, hold hands on the ice to "show the world that global warming is a myth." Coors sponsors.

FEBRUARY 6, 2024. University rescinds honorary degree. Angry UC Berkeley trustees "do this day cancel and delete" the posthumous honorary doctorate awarded to Beat author William Burroughs in 2031. The action is in response to recently discovered letters revealing that *Naked Lunch* was written on steroids and not, as previously claimed, on heroin.

FEBRUARY 19, 2103. Lunar "oldies" tragedy. All 114 members of an Elderhostel tour of the Mare Sinus Iridum are killed when their sled is hit by a Chinese test missile. The accident deals a death blow to the already ailing off-world tourism industry and leads many to question the moon's status as a free-fire zone.

FEBRUARY 12, 2116. First east-west winter solo kayak Atlantic crossing by a blind, gay, female graduate of an Ivy League college other than Yale. Guided by a wrist-beeper and buoyed by a rising tide, Hu-ling Hernandez Biddle (Princeton '09) paddles briskly into Montauk Harbor, where she is greeted by cheers from a crowd of six, two of them harbor police.

FEBRUARY 25, 2066. UN outlaws fluency gum. The popular chewing gum Chompsky, which provides several minutes of fluency in a wide variety of languages, is banned by the world body after a Ukrainian diplomat spits out a wad of Russian gum during a Security Council debate, nearly causing an international incident.

MARCH 4, 2232. Anglo-subsidence ends. The four-decades-long sinking of the British Isles comes to a formal conclusion as Charles IV steps onto a hovercraft and Ben Nevis disappears under the waves. California and Indonesia both offer sanctuary.

MARCH 12, 2026. Peace Corps sold. CNN buys the troubled agency for an undisclosed sum in a bid to compete with *Survivor* and *Fear Factor* for the lucrative reality TV market. Maria Schwarzenegger and Regis Philbin to co-host.

MARCH 21, 2012. Social Security reformed. The first 125 retirees, chosen by lottery, arrive by bus at the newly renovated Roosevelt Casino in Las Vegas, where each is presented with a hundred dollars in chips and a buffet ticket. The faux lobster is a hit.

MARCH 23, 5423. Gulliver returns under sail. The first intergalactic exploratory probe re-enters the solar system after a 2,216-year voyage. The info-mold aboard contains the first real-time pictures of our galaxy from outside. The only surprise is the size of the black hole at the center.

APRIL 1, 2005. Weapons of mass destruction found! The elusive casus belli, found buried in a breadbox by an alert young marine from Next Exit, Indiana, are positively ID'd by Saddam Hussein after less than 16 hours of nonlethal, extralegal interrogation. A matched set with faux pearl grips, the WMD are expected to fetch over $2,500 on eBay.

APRIL 1 – 30, 2917. One thousandth anniversary of Russian Revolution. The streets of Moscow are jammed by revelers from around the globe, kicking off a monthlong celebration honoring what is now recognized as the opening act of humanity's long, dramatic and ultimately successful struggle to bring Earth's resources under collective control.

APRIL 11, 2435. Last English speaker dies. Wilma Holder, of Grass, Oregon, the last native speaker of Central English, dies at age 81 of smoke inhalation after a cooking oil incident. Her enigmatic last word, "Clockwise!," which appears in no dictionary, leads to reams of speculation by linguistic antiquarians.

APRIL 26, 2074. World's "top" Internet café closes. Mountaineers mourn the loss of Tenzing's Tearoom in Everest's windswept South Col. Business at the café, known for its rancid yak butter tea and speedy broadband, fell off sharply after last year's near-record 1,121 Everest fatalities. Owners say the café will remain available for catered weddings.

MAY 4, 2018. Henry Kissinger dies in prison. The former Nobel Peace Prize winner, apprehended shivering and naked in an Aspen, Colorado, "spider-hole" in 2008, served only nine years of a life sentence for war crimes and crimes against humanity.

MAY 11, 2113. Last remnant of Amazon rain forest sold. A one-acre square of exotic plants, animals, birds and insects, sealed in a plastic bubble and protected by armed guards, sells on eBay for a record €255,000. Four years maintenance is included in the price.

MAY 23, 2087. Torture outlawed in US courts. In a shocking 5–4 reversal, the US Supreme Court declares duress confessions no longer admissible in federal courts. Prosecutors and rack manufacturers plan appeal to World Court in Beijing.

MAY 28, 2654. Nickel Moon falls. After two years of unsuccessful attempts to stabilize its orbit, Heavy Metal Resource Moon 212 falls into the Nevada Desert near the historic Vegas ruins. Popularly known as "Nickel Moon" because of its reflectivity, 212 was a favorite of lovers and romantics everywhere.

JUNE 5, 2387. Grass fire crosses 98th meridian. Ravaged Oglala and Texas both declare emergency as 1,500-mile flame front marches east toward Mississippi embayment.

JUNE 13, 2983. One thousandth anniversary of Pioneer 10, first man-made artifact to leave solar system. Hundreds of cheering chitinous larg raise a toast to the tiny spaceship that directed them to the planet that has since become their home. In a moving 11-second ceremony, a wreath is placed on the trench-grave of the 8.3 billion former inhabitants.

JUNE 22, 2031. Canada annexed. Citing "undisclosable security concerns," President Alma Gore exercises preemptive eminent domain to confer provisional statehood on the former British dominion. First new star on the flag since West Iraq.

JUNE 26, 2077. CEO falls to poison dart. Anne D. Lorey of Hershey-Ford, paralyzed while addressing a sales meeting, is the first victim of a blowgun gang targeting CEOs who make more than ten times as much as their lowest-paid employee. The "Whiffenpoof Boys" claim almost a hundred victims and kindle a new interest in corporate reform before they are apprehended.

JULY 4, 2013. Pot party on White House lawn. While drug dealers and police protest outside in a rare public display of unity, President Obama signs executive order officially ending the most destructive public health policy since Prohibition. Special guest ex-Pres Clinton inhales.

JULY 9, 2103. Last *New York Times* printed. Collectors and fishmongers line up in historic Times Square to get hard copies of the last edition of the world-famous daily.

JULY 14, 2789. Bastille Day anniversary. An estimated 125 million gather in Paris via holosim to celebrate the 1,000th anniversary of the Age of Democracy. Dick Clark hosts.

JULY 29, 2543. Stars go out. The entire visible universe, including the sun, goes dark for 3.4 hours, then mysteriously comes back on. Physicists speculate maintenance.

AUGUST 4, 2117. Lunar graffiti obliterated. A close pattern of six nuclear charges, fired by the Environmental Protection Agency, erases the 850-kilometer HE IS RISEN tag illegally etched into the Mare Insularum by suicide volunteers. Sierra International claims victory as protests rage in Oklahoma and Taiwan.

AUGUST 9, 2069. Apple sells Princeton. The cash-poor computer giant, still reeling from Hershey's edible iPod challenge, unloads the august Ivy League diploma shop for an undisclosed sum to a consortium of Chinese gaming moguls. Atlantic City included in deal.

AUGUST 18, 2025. Brits at it again. Oxford police use ultrasound batons to subdue unruly revelers at the 100th birthday party of SF author Brian Aldiss. The host, an OBE honoree, is charged with assault, imperial, after threatening an uninvited literary critic with the "business end" of a Hugo. Charges dropped at King's request.

AUGUST 26, 2117. R-H "retread" saves studio. The repro-holo remake of *Sideways* starring reBob Hope and reBing Crosby opens at #1 worldwide, ending a 12-year box office drought for troubled Cemetery Films. California winery stocks also soar.

SEPTEMBER 3, 2066. China buys atmosphere. Faced with new penalties for atmospheric dumping, the People's Republic of China purchases the atmosphere from troubled Oxxyon, prompting a fresh round of protests from Sierra Planetary, already contesting the Inuit sale of the Bering Sea to Saudi Arabia.

SEPTEMBER 9, 2104. Disneyland closed. The crime-ridden slum, home to vicious gangs of feral Micks, is electronically scourged by heli-police. Disneyland was once a world-famous destination for children of all ages.

SEPTEMBER 12, 2028. Hate crime punished. Two Vermont lesbians are jailed after their semipublic commitment ceremony (forbidden under federal hate crime statutes) is raided by lightly armed Christian Class Action volunteers. Both offenders lamed chemically in lieu of jail.

SEPTEMBER 23, 2201. Tsunami rolls over Long Island. An 80-meter tidal wave resulting from the eruption of Mount Pelée in the Caribbean washes all the way from Rockaway to Long Island Sound, killing over 20,000. Property loss, estimated at $3.9 billion, includes the Levittown National Heritage Village.

OCTOBER 7, 2020. Angry drivers jam DC beltway. Thousands of SUVs stop traffic to protest the new Greenecard required to buy gasoline. The brainchild of Transportation Secretary Lois Greene, the card contains a chip that adjusts the price on a rising scale. Thus, a driver who uses 25 gallons a week pays $4.22 for the first gallon and $16.04 for the 25th.

OCTOBER 11, 2356. Time "door" closed. The chrono rip accidentally opened by Phoenix University's runaway nuclear clock is sealed after complaints by American Dental Association that the singularity was being accessed illegally by graduate students seeking dental work.

OCTOBER 19, 2087. Rep missile goes awry. A Kurdish reparations missile, fired at Istanbul's Microsoft Tower, goes off course, destroying a popular amusement park in southern Cyprus. Reparations to follow.

OCTOBER 26, 2111. Highest peak on moon climbed. First ascent of 5,543-meter Mons Huygens (Mare Imbrium) by a team of four Chinese astro-alpinists and six Tibetan porters in "tight suits" with oxy wafers. The three-day (Earth calendar) assault followed the route of the ill-fated 2109 British expedition.

NOVEMBER 2, 2234. Prince Harold of Canada dies. The death of the 113-year-old Protestant patriarch sets off a power struggle as his 124 sons and daughters vie for control of their country's Taiga Reserve, which contains 55% of the world's fresh water.

NOVEMBER 9, 2047. Kennedy Slo-port opens in Midtown Manhattan. New York is the last major US city to require vertical take-off and landing capacity. The VTO facility atop the rebuilt Grand Central Station will accommodate two 500-passenger Boeing-China 897s at a time, thus finally ending the era of 150-mph-plus white-knuckle landings.

NOVEMBER 13, 2116. Last freshwater whale dies. The genetically modified mammals, formerly Earth's largest, were introduced to the Great Lakes at the beginning of the century in an attempt to save the species from the toxicity of the open seas.

NOVEMBER 21, 2007. First offshore nation recognized by UN. The 230-square-mile Nova Africa flotilla is centered around a former Carnival cruise ship, crowded with hurricane refugees, which was seized by its passengers and renamed the *Cinque* in 2006.

DECEMBER 2543. Mars moved. Scientists and developers rejoice as the Red Planet is field-folded into a one-AU orbit directly opposite Earth, where it is expected to develop a more hospitable climate. The controversial planetary repositioning is the most ambitious real estate project since Greece was terraced in the 23rd century.

DECEMBER 5, 2087. Lenin buried. Vladimir Ilyich Ulyanov, leader of the first Russian Revolution, is removed from Red Square and laid to rest beside his brother, Alexander, who was executed in 1887 for attempting to assassinate Tsar Alexander. Tsar Nick4 delivers eulogy.

DECEMBER 12, 2106. Intelligent design confirmed. The discovery in a Wyoming shale bed of a fossilized demon carrying a to-do scroll silences the last fanatical adherents of Darwin's archaic theory while disappointing those attributing ID to a benevolent deity.

DECEMBER 24, 2059. First contact. A 12-kilometer-wide saucer, thought at first to be an approaching asteroid, goes into low polar orbit around Earth. Attempts to communicate are unsuccessful.

JANUARY 1, 2206. New hue debuts. Merain™, a new primary color, is introduced by Newbisco's Crayola division. The copy-protected hue, which can be viewed but not reproduced without permission, prompts protests from artists and designers worldwide.

JANUARY 9, 2054. Enter Jane Bond. Alice Nduma of Duggin-town, Botswana, is named the new 007 by HeavensGate Studios. Slated to star in the upcoming *Girls Don't Cry*, Nduma is the first female and the first African to be cast in the classic role, traditionally dominated by white men.

JANUARY 19, 2060. Saucer zaps files. A sudden electromagnetic tone emanating from the mysterious 12-kilometer-wide saucer orbiting Earth erases 100% of the world's digital records. Panic on Wall Street. Attempts to communicate are unsuccessful.

JANUARY 23, 2124. Swimmer reaches North Pole. Scott Briley, the popular Olympic breaststroke brass medalist, conquers the slushy midwinter Arctic Ocean without a wet suit, thus claiming Grey Goose Vodka's €10,000 Northern Lites prize.

FEBRUARY 3, 2106. CIA prison found on moon. Chinese helium-3 prospectors discover the century-old ruins of a clandestine extraordinary rendition facility, complete with human remains and interrogation apparatuses. Congress demands inquiry.

FEBRUARY 12, 2076. Chickens block highway. Thousands of Free Range™ chickens, blown into drifts by a winter storm, stop traffic for six hours on I-95 near Baltimore. The traffic snarl leads to renewed calls for fencing the bioengineered birds, born without feet or wings.

FEBRUARY 22, 2060. Mystery saucer submerges. The huge alien saucer, which has silently orbited Earth for almost a year, descends and disappears under the Indian Ocean, causing a two-foot tsunami and worldwide governmental anxiety. All attempts to communicate with the enigmatic 12-kilometer-diameter craft have so far been unsuccessful.

FEBRUARY 27, 2265. Maglev tower falls. The 622-meter Humanities Tower at Alaskan Airways University, the world's tallest unsecured magnetic structure, collapses, causing the deaths of 11 tenured professors and 873 undergraduates and adjuncts. Migrating brownout blamed.

MARCH 3, 2123. Biopreds attack Cincinnati. Thousands of engineered predatory neoreptiles, recently escaped from a West Virginia bioweapons research facility, emerge in southern Ohio. Panic ensues as the fast-evolving preds haul themselves out of the water on rudimentary legs to feed on slow-moving Ohioans.

MARRR 09, 15432. Londinium updug. Te reman d'bigbig twonortowns i'dis cover an undug nexcoast of Uropea Guran, prom all happiness forcause London o Londionium, makelods oldpeopel where faddermudders mak remember. Ope air much of stone.

MARCH 24, 2032. March madness. A malfunctioning RoboRef™, apparently upset by catcalls, charges into the stands during a close Duke-UK game, killing four Kentucky Wildcats fans and injuring a security guard. Game goes into overtime; NCAA promises postseason investigation.

MARCH 24, 2066. Presidential first. An innovative noninvasive laser procedure, performed between a press conference and a state dinner, makes L. K. Cranmer the 53rd male US president, the third female president and the first chief exec to undergo gender-affirming surgery in office.

APRIL 16, 2120. Faulty arms award. Janet Ergastus, the recipient of the first cosmetic arm grown from nano-remobilized vestigial ("junk") DNA, is awarded $212,750 for career impediment. The plaintiff, a swimsuit model who amputated her left arm to get rid of tattoos, sued when it grew back covered with coarse hair and extending well below her knee.

APRIL 18, 2465. Windstorm on moon. Globik Underprize's celebrated lunar reclamation project turns disastrous when the "sticky-air" generator kicks off a 200 kph permanent global dust storm. The moon's features will not be seen again from Earth until 2499, when the low-grav designer gas is siphoned off into space by PlanetPump, a Halliburton subsidiary. Meanwhile, lovers mourn.

APRIL 23, 2048. European Israel recognized. A century of conflict in the Middle East ends as the state of Israel is reestablished on territory ceded in a historic reparations settlement by Poland, Germany and Ukraine. Arabs and Jews alike send congratulations from Democratic Palestine as the new state is admitted to the UN.

APRIL 28, 2066. Mystery saucer departs. The gigantic alien spaceship that orbited Earth for two years and then disappeared under the Indian Ocean suddenly emerges from the North Atlantic and speeds off into interstellar space, leaving huge sinkholes in Alaska, Arabia and Oklahoma. Tulsa and Riyadh are relocated when it is discovered that the saucer, swollen to four times its arrival size, took all the Earth's oil deposits with it.

MAY 1, 2052. Seattle rioters torch holy books. Hate Squad peacekeepers attack with soothe foam as Secular Party May Day marchers burn Korans, Bibles and *Dianetics* hardcovers, demanding an end to compulsory diversity readings in public schools. Three defilers killed, two sacred texts scorched.

MAY 19, 2201. Clone veep quits. Vice President Ralph Waldo Emerson, HC — the first historiclone elected to high office — resigns to become a HoloV talk show host. The controversial move is seen as a bid by the HBO-owned Democratic Party to challenge Johnny Carson, HC, the current late-night king.

MAY 23, 2041. New city for sex offenders. Neverland, Nevada, is granted first-ever adults-only municipal charter, giving convicted sex offenders a place to live. No Internet access.

MIDNIGHT, MAY 31, 2121. Time goes decimal. The 100-minute hour and the 100-second minute are officially adopted worldwide over protests by the International Olympic Committee (IOC) and the Tachometer Manufacturers of America (TMA).

JUNE 1, 2077. Coca-Cola™ retires. The one-time high-scoring NBA center turns in his jersey after a 20-year career. Coke, as he was known to his fans, was the first pro-baller to adopt a trademark name. His 99-point game record stood for 11 years until it was surpassed by Ford Explorer™ of the Google Lakers.

JUNE 22, 2060. Singularity cancelled. The 2060 solstice was to have been the day. An "actionably disappointed" Science Fiction and Fantasy Writers Association files a class action breach-of-promise suit against Disney, which bought the rights to the event from the Vernor Vinge estate for an undisclosed amount in 2033.

JUNE 15, 2252. Tragedy at Philly kitefest. A freak electrical storm kills 1,314, turning the 500th anniversary Franklin Day celebration into Philadelphia's worst public disaster since the 2012 gasoline riots.

JUNE 21, 2314. Last pope quits. Elizabeth P. Murran, known as Beth IX, abdicates the Vatican throne. Her termination settlement leaves the once wealthy Catholic Church reduced to three commercial properties in Rutlands, California, and a miniature golf course in Sicily.

JULY 3, 2063. New Confederate slaughter. Some 1,100 Civil War suicide reenactors, most of them from Virginia, blow themselves up to add realism to the 200th anniversary reenactment of Pickett's Charge. The annual Gettysburg gathering is a favorite of Civil War buffs.

JULY 4, 2076. July 4th BBQs banned. Intolerance marshals are placed on nationwide alert following a surprise presidential executive order declaring it a hate misdemeanor to "celebrate or commemorate" any political formation in which women are denied the vote.

JULY 19, 2205. Sailboat breaks ton. The *Silver Star* of Cornwall, England, EU, inserted into Hurricane Adeline by a chartered Chinese convict sub, is clocked at 101.43 knots before disintegrating. The knot is an archaic seagoing velocity measurement that approximates .5 meters per second.

JULY 24, 2217. Mars baby bids farewell. Charlotte Griddi, the first human born on Mars, dies at 121 in suburban Robinson. Griddi's televised birth in 2096 was witnessed by thousands back on Earth and almost a hundred on Mars. She is survived by her second and sixth husbands, hundreds of grandchildren, and longtime robot companion, Kim.

AUGUST 5, 2026. Marriage Amendment ratified. After a close vote in Kansas, the 28th Amendment is officially added to the US Constitution, specifying that matrimony must be between a man and a woman. It also forbids divorce and makes adultery a felony.

AUGUST 9, 2074. Tsunami shop opens. California's first commercial surf resort, featuring an oscillating undersea ultrasonic ram, draws surfers and protesters from around the globe. The so-called Malibu hammer, situated 10 miles offshore, can be felt as far inland as Bakersfield.

AUGUST 21, 2101. Chicago whale die-in. In an apparent mass suicide, thousands of genetically modified freshwater whales, designed and bred as an alternative fuel source, beach themselves on Chicago's Lake Michigan shoreline. Ethanol futures soar.

AUGUST 26, 2069. *Spirit* to come home. The early-21st-century Mars rover, found under a dune by an iron prospector, is sold to NASCAR for €99, plus shipping. It will be modified for use as a quarter-midget pace car.

SEPTEMBER 10, 2054. Burning Man statehood. Ratification celebrations (rat races) erupt at Black Rock City as 51st state prepares to select two senators via art car drags.

SEPTEMBER 15, 2035. DNR required for all over 70. Surgeon general's order heralded by health insurance execs. AARP expected to appeal.

SEPTEMBER 22, 2227. Gore Glacier burns. A careless camper is blamed for igniting the 280-square-mile Sierra aquastorage field, named after the 49th president. The century-old Thermosynth™ grid, the first of seven artificial glaciers installed in the California Snowpack Replacement Initiative, was riddled with dry caves and due to be replaced.

SEPTEMBER 29, 2187. Church of Scientology buys Old Navy. The purchase, prompted by the Garb Amendment extending religious tax exemptions to message tees, promises to give an edge to the troubled retail giant. Sales tax will still be charged on shorts and jeans.

OCTOBER 4, 2957. *Sputnik* millennial. Celebrants on four planets and three exvirons share holoceleb to honor the tiny satellite's launch by the Soviet Union in 1957. *Sputnik* was thought at the time to be the first man-made object in Earth orbit.

OCTOBER 11, 2044. Scarlet letter banned. A controversial new federal law prohibits all but convicted sex offenders from displaying the red X forehead tattoo, which has become popular with teens. ACLU and NAMBLA protest.

OCTOBER 21, 2465. Bermuda Triangle reappears. The infamous anomalous area, lost for 312 years, reappears in the South China Sea. Two US Coast Guard flyers are held for questioning after crash landing a P-38 Lightning on the rec deck of a Vietnamese oil platform.

OCTOBER 29, 2021. Theme bar tragedy. An oxygen flash fire in Universal's popular Saturn bar claims 65 victims, all lifetime members of the Science Fiction Writers of America, celebrating Universal's purchase of SFWA. No structural damage is reported.

NOVEMBER 3, 2957. Laika remembered. A ceremony in Crater Hong honors the 1,000th anniversary of the first multicellular bio-unit to orbit Earth. Laika was a Russian dog. Russia was a "nation" in N. Euron. The dog was a companion mammal to biohumans, several of which attend the ceremony in resurrection "suits."

NOVEMBER 14, 2031. Calendar copyright upheld. A surprise 32–12 World Court decision awards $124 billion in back royalties to C. Doctorow, the author-entrepreneur who used a little-known glitch in patent law to buy all rights to the Gregorian calendar in 2029 for $114 Canadian. Doctorow, currently homeless, admits that collection is "problematic."

NOVEMBER 19, 2155. Giant spider invasion. Giant spiders invade!

NOVEMBER 28, 2024. Apple unveils zPod. The thumbnail device uses a proprietary MP6 protocol, developed under license from NASCAR, that enables users to listen to 1,500 songs in six minutes. Steve Jobs explains the details in a 44-second speech at BeijingMacSnak.

DECEMBER 8, 2311. Twentieth-century menu sells for EA210,000 on eeeBay. "Chicken Wing" and "Shrimp Role Special" are among the fantastical delicacies depicted in four colors on glossy paperboard, purchased by Orson Kwan Pershing of Hong Kong, whose private collection of Chinese fast-food art has been profiled in both *Old Art News* and *Lookback Cooking* magazines.

DECEMBER 12, 2125. FDA approves streaming heart. The bio-plastic Daewoo mini turbine, which replaces the pulse of the archaic thumper with a constant-velocity flow, is expected to improve energy and memory while reducing danger of strokes and embolisms. Thousands sign up for the implant, and synth blood futures soar.

DECEMBER 22, 2011. Reindeer banned. TV pundit Bill O'Reilly dons antler hat in protest as UN Tolerance Court orders the Lapland herds destroyed "with all deliberate speed," citing their "unfortunate but undeniable" association with the out-lawed Santa icon.

DECEMBER 30, 2126. Taxi marathon thrills New Yorkers. Thou-sands cheer as 122 restored Checker and Chevy cabs, powered by reciprocating otto-cycle internal combustion engines, race from Jamaica Bay (former site of Kennedy Airport) to Times Square, commemorating the 100th anniversary of the day the last gasoline-powered taxi was pulled from the streets. Kenyan cabbie Obie Engami wins handily.

2007

JANUARY 1, 2111. Ball drops in Times Square. The draining and rehab of Midtown Manhattan continues apace with the reopen-ing of Times Square for the traditional New Year's celebration. The event, televised for viewers worldwide, has been simulated since the unfortunate and still undisclosed events of May 2X, 210X (ID).* Cheering hundreds in detox cloaks attend.

* HS interdict approved.

JANUARY 11, 2099. Sea turtle spotted. The environmental watchdog group Save the Sea Turtle announces a sighting near Catalina Island, California. The elusive only living sea creature was last seen alive off Guam in 2097.

JANUARY 21, 2066. Interneton nation joins UN. YouGoLand, population 58,740,356, is admitted to the United Nations by a 65–54 vote, Kurdistan and USA abstaining.

JANUARY 28, 2071. Evolution denier jailed. Greeneville, Tennessee, True Gospel minister Elmo "Mose" Hope is sentenced to 42 months in federal prison for distributing a pamphlet asserting that "God" created the Earth in six days and rested on the seventh. A 2069 federal law makes evolution denial a felony.

FEBRUARY 2, 2077. Age bias case settled. McDonald's is ordered to pay $91,000 in damages to 91-year-old Terry Glover of Grasp, Texas, who was fired four years ago because of a hand tremor that led to repetitive pricing errors. Glover thanks the court, evades the press and rides off on her antique BMW 1150 without comment.

FEBRUARY 12, 2333. Space elevator opened. The Clarke-orbit Rama Casino, formerly the exclusive playground of the superrich, is flooded with eager low rollers, thanks to Michelin's new living-fiber tether-lift, which is anchored near Franceville, Gabon.

FEBRUARY 19, 2105. Birth control call okayed. After months of testing, the FDA approves the controversial 900-94WOODY service that renders the caller sterile for 94 seconds. Cell phone sales surge. The €49.95 phone call works for men only.

FEBRUARY 26, 2023. Fantasy writers take early retirement. In an action hailed by fans and readers, 1,176 Sword and Sorcery writers turn off their word processors and leave the field, accepting an undisclosed four-figure mass buyout brokered by SFWA, Scholastic and the Magazine Publishers Association. The agreement is expected to return the crowded pulp genre to marginal profitability.

MARCH 3, 2021. Woman wins Best Actor. Cathy Clooney's Oscar for her role in *Killer Kiss* is the first female win since the Best Actress category was discontinued by the Academy as discriminatory. Clooney shares top honors with Shaheem Jefferson (Best Black Actor) and Lucia Rodriguez (Best Hispanic Actor). Billy Crystal hosts.

MARCH 5, 2105. Georgia Nessie runs amok. Atlanta's Fountain Square "monster" is returned to the manufacturer after devouring a wader, 8-year-old Clay Ballantine. The 20-meter bioengineered pond ornaments, sold and serviced by Inverness Amusements Ltd, normally feed on silicon meal.

MARCH 17, 2175. Lunar spa disaster. One hundred and twelve die when the popular Mare Nectaris Wellness Center is decompressed in a meteoric incident. The low-grav spa, built around the moon's only "hot" (4°C) spring, was originally opened as a Veterans Administration Rehab Center after the 2102 Gulf War.

MARCH 28, 2042. Stun gun pulled. The controversial XTC personal protection device, which distracts would-be assailants with a 33-second electrically triggered orgasm, is taken off the market after complaints of recreational use by teens.

APRIL 1, 2087. Traffic tie-up. Wind-scattered construction debris closes one lane on Houston's I-880 overpass, slowing rush hour traffic to a crawl for over an hour.

APRIL 9, 2107. Orbinauts go postal. Two killed, four injured in shoot-out aboard Singapore Space Station. The fatal six-hour laser battle, the worst since the low-orbit Valentine's Day massacre in 2085, prompts new calls for chemical castration of WASA personnel.

APRIL 22, 2023. Longest-missing child rescued. Bill Atwood-Helmers, kidnapped in 1993 by a renegade Cub Scout leader, is found clerking in a Lewiston, Idaho, liquor store. In a tearful reunion with his aging parents, who never gave up hope, Atwood-Helmers explains that his abductor threatened to take away his cell phone if he called police, mom or dad.

APRIL 24, 2055. World Bill of Rights approved. Modeled in part on the first 10 amendments of the US Constitution, the new 12-point document grants world citizens (humans) the same freedom to cross borders as trade, currency and capital.

MAY 1, 2104. Robot band wins May Day Prize. Controversy mars the ninth annual World Socialism Parade in Beijing as the solar-powered Harlem Dolls Marching Band takes top honors under protest from the all-bio Amazon Synchro Dance Ensemble.

MAY 11, 2165. Ice craft melts. The cruise ship *Dyson*, constructed in orbit from water ice and recycled sawdust, dissolves in a solar storm on its maiden voyage to Mars. All 610 souls aboard, including a Jersey Senior Scout troop, are lost.

MAY 18, 2026. This Month in History snags Pulitzer. The award for Historical Fiction is accepted by current editor Gavin Grant, who generously offers to share the honors with the founder of the series, whose name he unfortunately cannot recall.

MAY 24, 3109. Living autopsy. Med stocks soar as Kyser Helth announces a revolutionary new surgical procedure in which the patient is totally disassembled and reconditioned while partially conscious. Flat fee covers both parts and labor.

JUNE 3, 2209. Cghina gets moon. Thousands celebrate online as Sappho, assembled from cometary trash, is nudged into orbit by a sparkling fleet of hi-vac tugbots. The lightweight satellite will serve as a honeymoon station for the Gender Correction Society.

JUNE 11, 2077. Good day to die. The controversial Wyandotte Suicide Tower opens for business with 122 eager clients lining up to leap 100 meters to their deaths. The Wyandotte reservation also sells cigarettes and operates a casino.

JUNE 14, 2451. Digital Father's Day. World Wide Web shuts down for 24 hours to commemorate the 500th anniversary of UNI-VAC I, installed at the Census Bureau when biohumans were still subject to periodic counts. This is the first holiday called by the Internet itself.

JUNE 22, 2176. Old Faithful dies. Tearful tourists look on as the beloved Yellowstone geyser, failing since the 2171 Divide Quake, shows a last tepid plume and is pronounced dead by an EPA hydro-coroner.

JULY 2, 2081. Marathon tragedy. Hundreds die as flames sweep through the ranks of the Moscow Marathon. The deadly blaze, ignited by a cell phone spark, prompts new calls for a ban on "Everest Blood," the oxygen-rich synthetic circulatory medium popular with athletes and honeymooners.

JULY 4, 2058. A 51st state. The first new star in almost a century is added to the US flag as Urbana (Berkeley, Eugene, Austin, Ann Arbor and Woodstock) is officially granted statehood. The nation's first noncontiguous state will be governed by a five-person collective chosen by lottery.

JULY 23, 2076. Baby bust. The Lamarck Society's tax exempt status is revoked after six pregnant "volunteers" are forcibly evacuated from an undersea stress lab off Monterey, California. The controversial nonprofit claims to be developing a human that can breathe underwater.

JULY 29, 2254. Killer asteroid announced. Worldwide alarm as NC-1143.78, previously thought harmless, is found to be on a collision course with Earth. The impact of the Madeira-size stony body is expected to end all multicellular life on the planet on the morning of September 6, 2254.

AUGUST 3, 2088. Dorothy spins down. The mile-wide station-ary artificial tornado, Kansas's most popular (and only) tourist attraction since it was powered up in 2072 to attract and neu-tralize deadly dry line storm fronts, dissipates into scattered breezes after a suspicious torque field collapse. Enviroterror group Wild Skies claims responsibility.

AUGUST 5, 2019. Sasquatch road kill. A 7-foot, 310-pound hairy female hominid corpse is found on I-5 near Yreka, California, an apparent hit-and-run victim. Remains are held in the Klamath

County morgue pending settlement of conflicting claims by the Yreka Chamber of Commerce, the Smithsonian and the Native American Ancestry Council.

AUGUST 9–11, 2254. Asteroid-killer launch scrubbed. Gloom settles over a doomed Earth as the Chinese-American nuclear missile AK-50, aimed at the approaching 11 Nancy asteroid, misses its three-day launch window, delayed by a temporary injunction from the Islamo-Christian End Times Association. World Court issues regrets but defends the rule of law.

AUGUST 23, 2033. Sci-fi museum opens. Science fiction goes casual as tens turn out in jeans and tees for the humdrum opening of Seattle's new Mundane Science Fiction Museum. "Munds" (as the SF museum-goers call themselves) nod in approval as the main exhibit is unveiled: the actual rotary dial telephone seen in several classic SF films.

SEPTEMBER 4, 2104. Shasta blows. The first major Cascades eruption in over a century reduces the mountain to a 1,500-meter stump. Sixty-one climbers and two geologists reported dead or missing. Eight states blanketed with ash, including California, plan to sue North California for cleanup expenses.

SEPTEMBER 10, 2009. Whale attack. The ecotour boat *Melville* goes down off Provincetown, Massachusetts, after what survivors describe as a "coordinated assault" by a mixed pod of right and humpback whales. In retaliation, both species are dropped from endangered list.

SEPTEMBER 18, 2254. Lunar air rights protest. Thousands breathe free outside Burroughs Dome to protest Singapore's attempts to meter and sell the moon's new atmosphere. Singapore's claims date to September 6, when ice asteroid NC-1143.78 (or 11 Nancy), which was expected to annihilate all life on Earth, hit Singapore's Lunar ³H mine instead. The "sour but breathable" (*Off-World Adventure* magazine) atmosphere released by the impact is expected to last for several centuries before dissipating into space.

SEPTEMBER 28, 2056. Styx tour banned. Elderhostel's popular Charon Ferry Ride is shut down by the FDA, which claims that the one-way trip for 90s-only is an unlicensed euthanasia operation that practices age discrimination. Appeals are planned.

OCTOBER 4, 2022. Fog over Phoenix. With only Korea and Scotland abstaining, the UN votes 18 months of sanction fog over Phoenix, Arizona. The penalty in response to the 2020 "girly-goalie" riots is the most severe ever for a sports violation.

OCTOBER 10, 2113. Steam sling tragedy. One hundred five people and 34 dogs die as a container intended for orbit plows through a suburban Manila middle school. Pressure leaks in the Kīlauea geothermal catapult are blamed.

OCTOBER 14–20, 2065. Hummingbird die-off. Middle America's weeklong Fortean rain of tiny frozen corpses is traced to Homeland Air's promotional red-white-and-blue contrails, which apparently lured the birds to fatal altitudes.

OCTOBER 26, 2039. Habeas corpus reaffirmed. US Supreme Court rules that detainees must be released after seven years unless there is "actionable intelligence" linking them to a possible terrorist act. ACLU acting executive director Rita Maze hails victory from her open-air Guantanamo cage.

NOVEMBER 6, 2039. Endangered gorilla dies. The celebrated last mountain gorilla (*Gorilla beringei beringei*), dubbed Isha by naturalists, is found hanging from a banyan branch in a forest preserve near the Rwanda-Congo border, an apparent suicide.

NOVEMBER 10, 2024. Cyberpoet honored. Wordswork, the popular rhyming module self-generated from an anomaly in a web-based speech recognition system, is named Poet Laureate of Cyberspace by the Internet Endowment for the Arts.

NOVEMBER 13, 2116. Longest earthquake ends. The New New Madrid Tremor, which shook a three-state area for 18 months at an average of 6.7 (Richter), is declared subsided by the EPA. St. Louis and Memphis approved for salvage and resettlement.

NOVEMBER 27, 2012. Lunar X prize unwon. Google's $20 million prize, awarded for the first privately financed robotic rover landed on the lunar surface, is withdrawn when it is revealed that the winning Lunarian Ltd. "robot" was actually driven by a little person on steroids.

DECEMBER 12, 2321. Au revoir. Guy Depessant, the last native speaker of French, dies in a suburban Montreal nursing home at age 131.

DECEMBER 14, 2113. Suicide bomber reassembled. Annie Only, the rock militant who demolished the Hollywood Bowl during a Still Rolling Stones concert, is declared competent to stand trial after a dramatic 22-hour operation involving some 1,210 body parts of various sizes. The neuro-reanimated defendant is charged with the murders of 114 people, including herself.

DECEMBER 20, 2054. Google buys PaleoPic. The popular site that uses enhanced intergalactic photon echoes to display satellite images of Earth's ancient landscapes is acquired for an undisclosed sum rumored to be in the billions.

DECEMBER 25, 2077. Xmas greeting okayed. In a surprise US Supreme Court decision, the federal statute declaring nonecumenical holiday speech a hate crime is overturned 5–4. Merry Christmas!

2008

JANUARY 2, 2022. Record security payout. Estates and survivors of the 118 killed in the fusillade clearing the way for last year's Inaugural motorcade are paid $1,250 apiece, the largest such settlement since Blackwater was awarded the Secret Service contract.

JANUARY 4, 2253. Glacier to go. Argentina's Perito Moreno, the world's only remaining nonpolar free-range glacier, is acquired by Singapore's Natural History Museum for an undisclosed sum. Too large to ship safely, the 14-acre ice sheet will be melted and then reconstituted on-site.

JANUARY 22, 2114. Oldest patent upheld. The ancient Eridu-Sumer patent for the inclined plane, discovered on a clay tablet, is authenticated by the UN's Prior Claims Registry. Everyone on the planet is ordered to pay everyone else €.09.

JANUARY 28, 2065. Elvis blinks. The gigantic Plexiglas sunglasses are stolen from the "Welcome to Vegas" statue of Elvis Presley. The theft is thought to be in protest of the controversial New Vegas ordinance banning cardcounter shades.

FEBRUARY 11, 2065. Lethem Prize scandal. The €25,000 award for the year's best fully plagiarized novel is withdrawn under protest when it is revealed that portions of Emily Grant's *Tender Toll the Bells* were written by the author herself.

FEBRUARY 12, 2098. Cross cloud shredded. The Christian Coalition's controversial crucifix permacloud—a familiar feature in the skies over Washington, DC, since 2077—is destroyed by a fleet of suicide Cessna bombers. Disgruntled Darwinian holdouts suspected.

FEBRUARY 23, 2144. Jellyfish jams Golden Gate. Niptoon, the majestic free-range 1,420-square-kilometer bioengineered oil eater, which has fallen on hard times since the sea lanes were closed to tankers, is thought to be looking for food.

FEBRUARY 27, 2311. Pilgrim ship disaster. The Venus Colonization Society's *Mayflower* is lost with all 2,407 aboard when it ignites the terraformed planet's unstable new atmosphere on entry.

MARCH 4, 2021. Internet hammered. An estimated 40,000 websites are lost or damaged in cyberstorm Bruno, the worst since the Internet began generating its own weather. Banner ads ravaged in 90-plus pixel surge.

MARCH 9, 2133. Pluto disappears. The solar system's outermost and smallest planet is lost in space. Astronomers blame dark-matter patch.

MARCH 18, 2012. Snowbirds look south. Several million Mexican "illegals" are granted US citizenship in a reciprocal exchange with 12 million US seniors. Mexico's retirement village biz booms.

MARCH 25, 2065. Body farm deal. The University of Tennessee's famed experimental plot, where cadavers are left to decompose in the open for forensic study, is acquired by Horror Writers of America for an undisclosed sum. The 3-acre site will be used for a writer's retreat.

APRIL 1, 2008. *Locus* goes mundane. The glittery SF trade rag, recently acquired in a hostile takeover by Flatline Fantasy Ltd., announces that it will no longer review or accept ads for works that feature faster-than-light travel, wisecracking wizards or over-60 sex. Rudy Rucker cover cancelled.

APRIL 19, 2101. Pepper ants outlawed. The FDA bans the popular walk-on spice after months of often violent protests by PETA and the International Order of Waiters.

APRIL 21, 2022. Hate crime civil penalty. In a class action suit, the first of its kind, Princeton Black Studies emeritus professor Cornel West is penalized $1.3 million for his remark that "many whites are often racist." Four of his students will share the award with 127 million fellow Caucasians.

APRIL 29, 2065. Phone virus shuts Boston schools. The debilitating ringtone flu, which renders victims speechless for up to 24 hours, is thought by scientists to be the first virus to make the leap from digital to bio.

MAY 9, 2069. Polar bear hunt. Eager archers jam McMurdo's motel row for the opening of the first bow season for *Ursus maritimus*, which have decimated the local penguin population since they were airlifted to Antarctica after the melting of the arctic ice. Many hunters wear tuxedos in memory of the perky little birds.

MAY 11, 2164. Niagara falls. Hundreds cheer as a thin but continuous stream of water plunges over Canada's famed Niagara escarpment, soaking the rocks below. Torrential rains are credited for the flow, which lasts almost an hour.

MAY 19, 2123. Annie Farley birthday. The celebrated and eccentric inventor of the chrono ladder, now under UE interdiction, is born on this day in Indianapolis, Indiana—one of the eleven cities which, ironically, have banned any public mention of her extraordinary "time-saver."

MAY 14, 2044. Diana named queen. The late icon's divorce from then-prince Charles is retroactively declared invalid under England's new Sharia code. His Majesty King Charles and companion Heather will not attend the planned posthumous coronation.

JUNE 4, 2073. Disney dumps Windsor. The British royal family is sold to Virgin Atlantic for a sum rumored to be in the mid six figures, making VA the second-largest holder of EU monarchicals, after Yahoo.

JUNE 14, 2051. Binary holiday. Global travel, trade and communications shut down for 24 hours as computers take a worldwide personal day to celebrate the 100th birthday of UNIVAC I, powered up in Philadelphia in 1951.

JUNE 22, 2066. Teen band banned. The Grocery Boys, who play in a register that can only be heard by adolescents, are denied FM performance rights by the FCC after complaints that their Grammy-winning *Sounds Like Teen Spirit* makes certain household pets suicidal.

JUNE 23, 2212. Saturn disaster. Celebrity's *Lord of the Rings* is lost with all hands and 712 passengers in the worst cruise ship disaster since the solar sling opened the outer planets to tourism in 2192. Pilot error blamed.

JULY 3, 2126. Video postage issue. Popular new U-Vue stamps, celebrating the tenth anniversary of the Animal Rights Amendment, depict the now-extinct chicken, cow and pig in action. First day covers sell out by noon.

JULY 17, 1996. Airliner downed by meteor. TWA flight 800 is hit by a golf ball–size fragment of cometary trash off Long Island, New York. The tragedy is initially blamed on a fuel tank explosion.

JULY 22, 2077. Pirates go public. Pillage and Plunder's IPO levels off at a solid if unexciting €99 on NASDAQ. In a press release from its offshore office, the cooperative venture by Indonesian, Alaskan and Somali buccaneers promises "high risk, high returns and high adventure."

JULY 29, 2116. Court okays itself. Arguments that President Arlen-Ihowe has packed the Supreme Court with emergency appointments are rejected in a close 122–113 decision, with 11 justices abstaining.

AUGUST 4, 2022. Female first. Cheers and tears greet the historic unveiling of the first woman's face on Mount Rushmore, carried live on afternoon TV. In accordance with Oprah's Go Green initiative, her 20-meter-high likeness was carved with lasers rather than explosives.

AUGUST 11, 2069. Lights on! Apple-ABC's new plasma cannon gets rave reviews as the aurora borealis is seen for the first time in the summer months, and as far south as Cupertino.

AUGUST 22, 2044. Get out of jail free. The USA loses its prison population lead as 2,151,034 inmates are released in the largest amnesty since the Civil War.

AUGUST 23, 2176. Instant oil. British Petroleum's DinoHawk goes operational. The controversial fusion-powered micro singularity reduces landfill waste to usable petroleum in seconds. "Only problem now," says BP CEO Harrison Huong, "is getting it out."

SEPTEMBER 1, 2104. Speed golf win. PGA underdog Elmo Kardashian pars Pebble Beach in 27:11.4, besting Tiger Woods's 86-year world record by almost nine seconds.

SEPTEMBER 12, 2024. Stephen Hawking retires. In his televised farewell speech the famed physicist reveals that he has actually been dead for six years but wasn't done with his research projects.

SEPTEMBER 19, 3031. Earth off-limits. Catastrophic plate openings and boiling seas prompt "indefinite closure" of the planetary disaster park that has been a favorite destination of galactic adventurers since it was opened in 2855.

SEPTEMBER 26, 2033. Smoke break. In a close 5–4 decision, the US Supreme Court okays a last cigarette for death row prisoner Clarence Miggs. Smoking has been banned inside United States borders since 2017.

OCTOBER 1, 2123. Mecca replaces Greenwich. Muslims around the world rejoice and mapmakers mourn as the new prime meridian is made official.

OCTOBER 6, 2044. Teen torture okayed. Enhanced punishment techniques, previously forbidden in juvenile cases, are approved by the US Department of Prisons as "cruel but no longer unusual."

OCTOBER 22, 2108. Roomba recall. After a rogue Roomba is blamed for the gruesome deaths of two seniors who fell asleep on a shag rug, 155,000 of the popular free-range biovac house helpers are pulled from hardware and pet store shelves.

OCTOBER 29, 2064. Meet the beetles. Responding to a plea from Mayor Trump herself, the NYC Department of Health approves Crunch Crazy, the nation's first fried-insect fast-food restaurant, just in time for a Halloween opening. The tiny tasties prove especially popular with Times Square tourists.

NOVEMBER 4, 2046. First First Lady VP. Republican presidential candidate Clay Ordoman and his wife (and now vice president–elect), Anne, win in a landslide, promising to return family values to the White House.

NOVEMBER 11, 2114. Hadron goes belly-up. The Franco-Swiss waste-disposal giant, whose curbside micro decyclers have dominated the municipal refuse market for almost a century, files for bankruptcy. Hadron's stock has been sliding since São Paulo disappeared.

NOVEMBER 13, 2037. Hate crime conviction. Al-Qaeda's Commander Atif is sentenced in absentia to 11 months in jail because of remarks accompanying his recent nuclear attack obliterating Manchester, England.

NOVEMBER 19, 2066. No-road race win. Adam Unser, in a vintage Humvee, wins the Libertarian 3000 — the one-time-only, coast-to-coast auto race that avoids all public roadways — with an ET of just under six months.

DECEMBER 2, 2064. Biodiesel banned. Exxon's Orca™ loses its renewable classification with the sudden extinction of the sperm and right whales. Increased holiday traffic blamed.

DECEMBER 10, 2021. Malzberg spurns Nobel. Stunning the staid Swedish Academy, the celebrated author denounces as well as declines the newly established Nobel for Science Fiction (which includes a $1,500 cash award) in a fiery speech maintaining that SF is literature.

DECEMBER 16, 2025. Rushmore erased. South Dakota's first terrorist attack hints at an ominous new coalition between al-Qaeda, Earth First! and the American Indian Movement.

DECEMBER 27, 2141. Northern lights out. Indo-India's orbiting plasma-capture energy grid is blamed for the dimming of the auroral displays that have delighted arctic skygazers for centuries. Alaska, Iceland to sue.

2009

JANUARY 1, 2029. Hookers™ make Mac menu. Deep discounts on the farm-raised, naturally sweetened dessert parasites, already popular with weight watchers, are expected to boost sagging fast-food sales.

JAN 4, 2214. First new moon landing. Scotland's *Redgauntlet* touches down on Tiny Tim, the smallest of the three new satellites acquired by Earth during the 2199 Corburis asteroid near-disaster.

JANUARY 18, 2063. Cheerless Super Bowl. Fans boo halftime show after Raiders' Blaster Babes are banned. Burning body parts from the popular suicide cheerleaders are blamed for last year's tragic Denver stadium fire.

JANUARY 30, 2104. New #1 city. The UN's northwest African refugee camp officially passes both São Paulo and Beijing in population. According to the monthly satellite census, the 11,500-square-kilometer tent metropolis, which has no permanent buildings, mail service, restaurants, schools or name, is now home to 44.8 million.

FEBRUARY 4, 2032. LDS Amendment. Disappointed gay rights groups blame "Mormon money" for the narrow passage of a constitutional amendment defining marriage as between "a man and any number of women."

FEBRUARY 11, 2114. "Crap gas" ban. Overriding a joint US-Israel veto, the World Congress prohibits civilian use of C-330, the military assault gas that renders crowds incontinent.

FEBRUARY 21, 2088. Terminix bailout. Congress grants the GE subsidiary, which has the exclusive contract for all executions in the United States, a $2 billion bridge loan. Last year's Supreme Court ruling limiting mass executions to 100 (thus raising unit costs) is blamed for the revenue shortfall.

FEBRUARY 24, 2205. Twister rescue. The 2,100-kilometer leptonplasma High Plains Storm Wall, credited with saving hundreds of lives since it was powered up in 2195, is destroyed overnight in an apparent terrorist attack. Save the Tornado, a militant offshoot of Earth First!, claims responsibility.

MARCH 5, 2105. Shark attack. Santa Cruz's ecofriendly image suffers as poly sharks devour a dozen surfers in one day. The 2-ton plastivores, bioengineered to feed on coastal trash, are thought to have been after the wet suits, not their wearers.

MARCH 14, 2027. Equal rights victory. Philip Seymour Hoffman wins his third Oscar and second Best Actor for his starring role in *Robeson*. In his acceptance speech he thanks the Academy for banning racial casting.

MARCH 19, 2435. Middle East mud volcano. Tourists, worshippers and disputants flee as a crown of hot mud covers Jerusalem, ending 25 centuries of conflicting claims.

MARCH 27, 2083. Roadway buyout. In a move that rocks Wall Street, the Department of the Interior buys the interstate highway system from Schwab-Nabisco's troubled White-Line division. Congress decries "socialism" and promises hearings.

APRIL 1, 2063. Empire State Building lost. A container ship disaster off the Cape of Good Hope sends New York's beloved landmark to a watery grave. The legendary skyscraper, boxed and numbered for reconstruction, was to have found a second life as a vertical mall in Jakarta.

APRIL 3, 2047. First 4D hit. *The Oregon Trail* rakes in record opening numbers, benefiting from Dreamwarps-Oreo's proprietary new chronospecs that allow viewing of a 4-hour film in 20 minutes.

APRIL 17, 2465. Arctica™ opens. Powered by core-deep thermal reversers, Brazil's newest reality attraction recreates conditions at the end of the last ice age (circa 20°C), complete with polar bears, penguins and helpful Eskimos™. The cool new park is expected to draw some of the overflow from nearby Amazonia™.

APRIL 22, 2287. Kilimanjaro collapses. Natives, naturalists and English majors mourn as Africa's loftiest peak is leveled by a controlled nanonuclear implosion. The demolition of equatorial mountains (described as "drawing in the skater's arms") is part of an international effort to speed up Earth's rotation to compensate for the slowing caused by the proliferation of windmill farms worldwide.

MAY 4, 2011. GM back on top. After a terrifying brush with bankruptcy, General Motors takes the lead again as the world's most popular, most profitable and most innovative automaker. Critics and fans agree, it was the '09 Camaro that did it!

MAY 11, 2104. Alien craft uncovered. The UN's SETI Institute salvage team releases dramatic photos of an extraterrestrial spaceship found embedded in Antarctic ice. The ship, which is estimated to be over 425,000 years old, is 1.23 meters long.

MAY 14, 2055. *Austen vs. Byron* opens on Broadway. The reality musical, based on the novelist's recently discovered Mediterranean journal, tells of her "more poetic than fictional" collaboration with the clubfooted poet. Lukewarm critics no obstacle as the show begins a record-breaking 22-year run.

MAY 23, 2076. Copyshop acquires eBay. In a surprise hostile takeover, 1.5 million shares of the Internet giant are seized by a Lagos neighborhood copyshop. The surrendered stocks were being held as collateral for a cash transfer from the widow of a deposed Nigerian finance minister.

JUNE 2, 2745. *Bounty* phones home. Incoming is finally received from the manned interstellar probe, feared lost for over five centuries. The message, described by biolinguists as a "boastful lament," is said to be from the ship's plants.

JUNE 12, 2015. Torture not torture. Denying a historic joint ACLU–al-Qaeda appeal, the US Supreme Court frees both Cheney and Rumsfeld, overturning their World Court conviction and affirming their claim that torture is, in fact, not torture.

JUNE 20, 2076. eBay shuts down ID sales. Commerce Department officials, alarmed by the spread of multidentities, are seeking a ban on Facebook swaps as well. Some people are said to hold scores of identities while others go without.

JUNE 28, 2104. Somali pirates seize UN. The 190-meter-long blue-flagged *Deliberative Princess* is boarded by armed brigands off Bajuni. Secretary-General Samuel Caesar, held hostage on the bridge of the converted cruise ship, calls for calm in response to the worst crisis since the embattled Congress of Nations lost its New York lease and was forced offshore.

JULY 2, 2061. Sea boils bears. Alarmed by a late thaw, Russian geo-engineers blast open a subpolar thermal vent to open the Arctic Ocean to summer shipping. Greenpeace-Sierra charges ecocide.

JULY 12, 2029. White House debuts A-phone. President Pelosi is the first to try GE&E's new cell-to-cell phone that enables conversation with Alzheimer's sufferers. After a call to Senator Kennedy, she declares the experience "unforgettable."

JULY 21, 2109. Tsunami hits the Bruce. Thousands die as a 70-foot wall of water, set off by a Canary island landslide, washes over the crowded Springsteen City boardwalk and inundates casinos.

JULY 29, 2077. Apple stock replaces dollar. In a controversial move protested by both Wall Street and Beijing, the IMF calls in greenbacks for fixed-rate replacement. New jobs currency soars against euro and yen.

AUGUST 4, 2076. *Plastic Man* breaks through. Thousands cheer as the 3,400-ton Japanese slurge-breaker enters Pearl Harbor—the first vessel to reach Oahu since the mid-Pacific plastigyre blocked all sea traffic in late 2068.

AUGUST 8, 2015. Amy Upson-Treen born. The author, who will win two Pulitzers, four Hugos and a Claret for her handicapped vampire psychic detective series set in ancient Rome, *Precinctus IV*, weighs 6 pounds, 11 ounces.

AUGUST 15, 2069. Woodstock 100th anniversary reenactment. Half a million pay $500 a head to romp naked to soft rock in synth-mud, stoned on LSD and marijuana supplied by local Lutheran churches; 12 teens arrested for smoking cigarettes.

AUGUST 23, 2028. Bird strike. Nationwide, 22 airports, including LAX, O'Hare and LaGuardia, are closed for 10 hours as cranes and pelicans mass on runways in an apparently coordinated effort.

SEPTEMBER 2, 2019. Stern snags Mac. Radio personality Howard Stern's sagging ratings soar as his MacArthur "Genius Grant" is announced. Other honorees include a clown and a traffic cop.

SEPTEMBER 12, 2066. Lincoln Center live birth. The first US performance of Paolo Puccilini's controversial *Aurora*, which features a second-movement onstage delivery by the first soprano, receives critical raves. It's a boy.

SEPTEMBER 22, 2043. Kindle controversy. Authors Guild and Salinger estate join Marlboro to protest new Kindle, which auto-deletes all references to smoking in downloaded fiction. Amazon claims health benefits.

SEPTEMBER 28, 2116. New star in flag. Nationwide cybercelebrations as Internet officially becomes the 51st state. Senatorial avatars Luka3 and KrispyKritter seated without incident as House awaits broadband installation.

OCTOBER 9, 2155. Moby-Dick and -Jane spotted. The celebrated pair of 400-meter bioengineered "green" whales, released by Exxon Biofuels in 2149, are seen off Cape Verde trailed by three calves. Whale oil futures soar.

OCTOBER 19, 2104. Singapore buys Venice. The legendary Renaissance city, abandoned after the 2089 Mediterranean hypercane, will be reconstructed as the centerpiece of Southeast Asia's new Scuba Duba Water Park.

OCTOBER 23, 2048. Michael Jackson dies. The reclusive King of Pop, who faked his death in 2009 to rejuvenate his sagging career, is found dead in his elegant Dubai "playhouse" at 89. There are no survivors.

OCTOBER 25, 2066. AuralZap hangs up. The dial-up cosmetic surgery service, specializing in phone-delivered "voice jobs," is closed by federal court order after clients are linked to the recent rise in speech-keyed auto thefts.

NOVEMBER 12, 2073. Sitka Sal convicted. Alaska's notorious Inland Passage pirate chieftain, who scuttled 11 ships before she was captured, is sentenced to life in prison without health care.

NOVEMBER 22, 2412. New moon. The lunar backside is fully visible from Earth for the first time, due to a 2387 meteor strike that set the moon into slow rotation.

NOVEMBER 24, 2088. FDA okays BioMite. Procter & Gamble's controversial intestinal paragene, which gives consumers the ability to eat wood, is approved for sale to seniors and foreign markets.

NOVEMBER 29, 2212. Lady Liberty located. The Statue of Liberty, missing since the 2198 Wall Street riots, is located in a Queens warehouse once used by the NYPD for evidence storage.

DECEMBER 5, 2053. Kluny™ for kids! Secretary of Childhood Kitty Arnason, America's first cabinet-level minor, celebrates her sixth birthday by lifting age restrictions on the replipilatory face cream that gives men (and women) a three-day beard for up to six hours.

DECEMBER 11, 2067. Disney-Marvel buys Vatican. Savior's new superhero status is predicted to revive interest in the once-popular religion. Bethlehem Birthday Bash to feature orbital nano-nova display.

DECEMBER 13, 2204. Water-eater ID'd. A .002-millimeter black hole, located off Catalina Island, is blamed for the recent six-foot drop in sea level worldwide. The nano singularity was apparently created accidentally during the audiovoxing of the 4D Higgs-Hadron musical *Divinity Will Do*.

DECEMBER 22, 2121. Bernie walks. Bernard Madoff, convicted of financial fraud in 2009, is released with "good time" after serving only 112 years of his 150-year sentence. The legendary Ponzier attributes his longevity to dietary supplements. Descendants of victims protest as shark-fin futures soar.

2010

JANUARY 1, 2706. Chronosphere cracked. The first live time capsule is opened on schedule in Athens after 500 years. The nine chrononauts, who experienced the centuries as 126 months, are said to be in good health but not speaking to one another.

JANUARY 1, 2103. Suicide concert scratched. The annual New Year's performance of Hannah McHannah's *Glock #9*, which calls for the conductor to shoot herself midway through the third movement, is cancelled when NYC rescinds Carnegie Hall's pistol permit. NRA, NEA and Ticketmistress file joint suit.

JANUARY 19, 2098. EU bans Blueblood™. The synthetic circulatory medium, originally developed for horses and popular with cyclists, eldertourists and stand-up comics, is found to be poisonous to Carpathia's endangered bats.

JANUARY 24, 2065. "I Do" Inc. Google weds Apple in the first major merger since corporations were awarded full personhood rights in 2063. Rabbi Bunny Mei Ling performs the marriage ceremony, which is expected to render the Fed's most recent antitrust ruling moot.

FEBRUARY 2, 2435. Jupiter implodes. The recent proliferation of wildcat dark vapor mines is blamed for the sudden, spectacular collapse of the gas giant, once the system's largest. EUM promises regulatory review.

FEBRUARY 15, 2064. Galileo Day. In a dramatic commemoration of the celebrity heretic's 500th birthday, two astronomers chosen by lottery are burned at the stake live on HuluFox.com. The event is FCC-certified fair and balanced, since one astronomer is an opponent and the other an adherent of the controversial heliocentric theory.

FEBRUARY 18, 2134. Seeing stars. Millions turn out in Europe and America for the first look at extralunar worlds since the last century's subarctic peat fires opaqued the upper atmosphere. Big Dipper a big favorite in the three-hour display caused by freak jet stream activity.

FEBRUARY 22, 2113. AZ ♥ Mexico. After a closely monitored plebiscite, Arizona becomes the fourth state to annex out of the USA. Education, health care, Mexico's booming economy all factors in the landslide vote. MN Canada and FL Cuba send congrats.

MARCH 7, 2028. Oscar turns 100! Spike Lee and Parker Posey share Lifetime Achievement honors in the hour-long Academy Awards centennial, hosted live on Facebook by a polished Cher II. Best Picture goes to *Graveyard of the Dead*, the first unanimated 2D win since *Lulu's Vagina* in 2021. There is said to be a party after.

MARCH 9, 2144. Quake shakes Stockholm. Swedish Republic sues for peace after a two-hour niner (RS 9.4), unleashed by the EU's elite Borehole Brigade, flattens the capital from below, ending the outlaw regime's bid for subarctic supremacy.

MARCH 14, 2045. Johnston-Palin quits. After barely one year in office, America's first Alaskan veep resigns to fill the *Tonight Show* slot opened by Oprah's embarrassing on-air Alzheimer's episode. His grandmother was once a vice-presidential candidate.

MARCH 27, 2073. Quad wins Daytona. Injured NASCAR vet "Pokey" Pearl takes the checkered flag in a near-record 2:53:19, after leading for 66 of 200 laps. The popular paralyzed hotshoe attributes his victory to his "awesome" pit crew, his "streakin" Kia lectric and NASCAR's last-minute ruling that the driver does not have to actually be *inside* the race car.

APRIL 1, 4132. Universe recalled.

APRIL 4, 2032. Castro burns. Rioters rage through San Francisco's historic gay ghetto, protesting the reparations draft of out homosexuals between 18 and 58, designed to compensate for all the years they missed military service.

APRIL 12, 2055. "Good night and good luck." The cruise ship *Orbital Princess* goes dark as rescue hopes fade to black. The live broadcasts from the stricken craft, featuring cannibalism and a dramatic weekly voting ritual, enjoyed the highest Nielsens since *Survivor*.

APRIL 23, 2154. First contact. Earth's ants greet humans and promise peaceful coexistence. The newly conscious planetwide superorganism, dubbed "Auntie Meme" by an eager press, is apparently the result of a 100-million-year gestational process.

MAY 3, 2032. Age change okayed. In a surprise 5–4 decision, the US Supreme Court rules that birthdate is as subject to personal choice as name, sex and religion. Medicare braces for biggest rush since organ donors were granted full benefits in 2029.

MAY 12, 2246. "Told you so!" MIT's 4D quantum chronotriangulator confirms that our universe was created by an unauthorized (and ill-advised) experiment that went wrong exactly 6,394 years ago. Bible sales soar.

MAY 26, 2021. Somali pirates release Staten Island Ferry. NYers cheer and some grumble as Mayor Rebecca Maldonado hands over the undisclosed ransom, rumored to be in excess of $11,500.

MAY 29, 2103. Diversity pays. Broadway's controversial new Sharia Theatre opens with a smash hit revival. *On-Stage* blog-zine raves that Miriam Hassan's full-burqa portrayal of Blanche "restores primacy to Tennessee Williams's script."

JUNE 1, 2048. Same-sex wedding compromise. Caterers and couturiers celebrate as Teas and Dems announce last-minute June waiver requiring one party to buy, but not necessarily wear, a dress.

JUNE 13, 2298. Satellite snags Booker. Simon & Comcast's orbital *AlgoRhythm IV*, which auto-assembles global e-media scraps into genre bestsellers, was directly over Udder-Pinwick, Sussex, when the prizewinning *Murder by Weapon* was downcast. Authors Guild objects.

JUNE 21, 2108. Lunar casino closed. Mare Opprobrium's most popular destination, Aces Over, is decertified after court-ordered DNA tests reveal that Neil Armstrong was not, as claimed, 1/34 Lakota.

JUNE 29, 2055. High seas slowdown. The UN Ecommission's controversial 4.5-knot speed limit on all internally powered shipping vessels is expected to reduce air and underwater noise pollution and perhaps lead to a new Age of Sail.

JULY 4, 2105. Placebo™ approved. Stem cell futures soar as FDA okays the compact new accessory organ developed by Cellgro's bio-gen team. The eagerly awaited autoimmune upgrade is expected to outsell even GE's wildly popular RadioLarynx™.

JULY 16, 2049. Pope weds. Taking dramatic advantage of recent doctrinal adjustments, Lou the Eleventh exchanges vows with sultry Portuguese pop star Mariana Oveida as a stunned

College of Cardinals applauds politely. It's Oveida's third marriage; the pontiff's first.

JULY 24, 2065. Swipe wipes night sky. Heartland bids stars farewell as the controversial stratospheric ozone shroud is uploaded by the Red State Alliance to kick off its Heliocentric Revival.

JULY 27, 2025. iPad snags Salinger. The reclusive author's massive posthumous fantasy tetralogy, *It's a Wise Wizard*, commands a record $11.6 million after a tense nine-day bidding war with Amazon.

AUGUST 9, 2119. Citizen ship sails. One hundred twentieth-eighth Amendment to US Constitution is ratified, making citizenship renewable annually for a fee of $2,150. Discounted INS family package available through Amazon.

AUGUST 14, 2101. First flyer bicentennial. Celebs gather in Fairfield, Connecticut, to commemorate Gustave Whitehead's acetylene-powered Airplane 21, the first manned heavier-than-air craft to sustain level flight. Two Ohio bicycle engineers were previously credited with the achievement.

AUGUST 23, 2274. Agg welcomes homesteaders. The artificial planet, constructed of asteroidal debris and maneuvered into one-AU cross-solar orbit, is officially opened for settlement. First 11,500 settlers chosen by lottery disembark to brass band.

AUGUST 26, 2032. Camel Caravan cancelled. Winston-Salem's popular smoking film festival is closed after two teens are discovered in audience for *Breakfast at Tiffany's*.

SEPTEMBER 2–14, 2144. Lost days found. The 11 days lost in the 1752 transition from the Julian calendar to the Gregorian are discovered, wrapped in rotting canvas, by a curator-intern in the Diana Annex of the British Museum. Royal family claims ownership.

SEPTEMBER 10, 2043. Wall Street walks. Trading shuts down as bank and brokerage execs protest "socialistic" Fed edict limiting personal salaries to 1.9 million times minimum wage.

SEPTEMBER 22, 2018. Lucy Webster-Lang birthday. The first transgender US Supreme Court justice is born Ben Webster in Alliance, Nebraska.

SEPTEMBER 13, 2218. Alien fleet sighted. ETA for the nine 1,600-meter rhomboidal vessels heading earthward at .77c is December 2765.

OCTOBER 9, 2124. "Franklin" falls. Northeast power grid darkens as Philly Electric's stratospheric jet stream turbine plunges into Delaware Bay. Tether failure blamed.

OCTOBER 11, 2021. Dino apology. In a dramatic appearance on Fox's *Earlier Show*, Vice President Palin apologizes to the dinosaurs for blaming them for global warming. It has been known since the late 20th century that most oil deposits formed from oceanic microorganisms.

OCTOBER 21, 2045. SS Reform Act passed. After a bitter floor battle, the Senate passes a new Social Security bill aimed at closing the deficit. The controversial law denies federal highway funds to states that allow seniors to wear seat belts.

OCTOBER 22, 2031. Oil attack. Baltic states brace for toxic disaster as Islamic militants scuttle a 120,000-ton tanker with open hatches 8 kilometers off Gdańsk. Web cartoonist blamed.

NOVEMBER 9, 2103. TETI stops listening. Citing personnel problems, the EGA's elite alien contact team abandons efforts to talk directly with the visiting Yyfraa. Like us, the Yyfraa communicate by expelling waste, but they emit it from the digestive rather than the respiratory system.

NOVEMBER 11, 2155. Ian Rodriguez birthday. The discoverer of Jupiter's celebrated floating scrolls is born in suburban Hyperion, Ohio. His 11 dramatic reports from the Great Red Spot are credited with the revival of Judaism worldwide.

NOVEMBER 23, 2074. Steamliner lost. United's eco-flagship *Polar Princess*, a 1,350-seat nuclear-powered Boeing 919, goes down over Bering Sea with no survivors. Boiler explosion blamed in history's worst air tragedy.

NOVEMBER 28, 2035. Talking dog dies. *Hey There* late-night talk show followed Leno for twelve years. The canine host was known for his warm, humorless personality and support for human rights. Owner Gentech to issue memorial mug.

DECEMBER 4, 2018. Slavery abolished. Responding to complaints from parents, the Texas legislature prohibits the use of the word "slavery" in textbooks. The new approved terminology is "assisted living."

DECEMBER 11, 2105. Moyld™ reaches Chicago. Mayor Annaya declares emergency as the corn-based biopavement spreading from DowAgro's Decatur lab shuts down South Side malls and interchanges. The sponge-like mat has grown exponentially, covering almost 15,000 square kilometers since its October escape.

DECEMBER 16, 2024. Tea Party Day. Bypassing congressional protests, outgoing President Beck declares the anniversary of the 1773 Boston protest a national holiday for all except federal employees.

DECEMBER 28, 2207. Rings wrecked. A direct hit by a 1,200-meter asteroid scatters Saturn's famous rings. The six-minute event is a favorite on U2b.

2011

JANUARY 2, 2034. Heroism pays. First contractor Medal of Honor winner, L. W. "John" Wayne, receives million-dollar treasury bond in White House ceremony. His now-famous ride will be the subject of an upcoming Scholastic special.

JANUARY 7, 2096. Gulf boom breaks. Northern Europe braces for toxic disaster as an ocean of oil-soaked industrial slurge, released by hypercane Xena, enters the Gulf Stream. The failure of the Florida-Yucatan surface dam raises new concerns about the use of the Gulf of Mexico as a waste pool.

JANUARY 13, 2209. Tycho burns. The flash fire that destroyed the domed lunar prison, killing 6,488 in less than 11 seconds, is thought to have been ignited by a flint micrometeorite striking a convict's steel shovel.

JANUARY 26, 2107. Halley's captured. The celebrated comet, nudged into a patented solar synchronous orbit by Dreamcatcher Entertainment, will now appear annually during the People's Choice Awards.

FEBRUARY 4, 2014. Crucifixion okayed. In a 5–4 decision, US Supreme Court rules "enhanced punishment" justified for crimes in which children or public safety endangered.

FEBRUARY 16, 2322. Armada arrives. The nine-vessel alien fleet first sighted in 2218 enters solar system 400 years ahead of schedule. Sudden appearance in Kuiper Belt suggests space-time fold. First contact attempts fail.

FEBRUARY 18, 2032. Nobel for Assange. Ignoring US protests which caused a two-month delay, the Committee of Five awards the Nobel Peace Prize to WikiLeaks founder Julian Assange. It is the first time a Guantanamo inmate has been so honored.

FEBRUARY 21, 2105. Smartpipe eats school. Panic strikes Wilma, Indiana, as an elementary school is sucked underground by a rogue natural gas pipeline. The self-repairing bioconduit was apparently seeking glue.

MARCH 3, 2276. Moon gets moon. The surprising lunar capture of Cruithne (NEA 3753) has physicists scrambling to revise Newton's "laws." The 5-kilometer-diameter step-satellite, dubbed Crew, will inspire a new generation of speed astronomers.

MARCH 11, 2087. Death jet lands. Air India's flight 256 arrives at Heathrow's gate 6 with no survivors of the electrical fire that asphyxiated 223 passengers and crew. The tragic on-time arrival is credited to Airbus's new SansCap autopilot.

MARCH 20, 2044. Lectron recall. GM's popular nuclear-powered steamer is recalled after a rush hour fender bender forces a mass evacuation of downtown Rock City (formerly Cleveland), Ohio. NASCAR mulls lectron ban.

MARCH 24, 2021. Oscar shoot-out. Disappointed screenwriters open fire with automatic weapons as Best Screenplay award goes to Amazon's Kindlewriter Deluxe for *Old Fockers*. No injuries as shots were wild.

APRIL 3, 2143. Mars hero mourned. E. Benn-dire, the first human to set foot on the Red Planet, dies at 112 in her Cairo townhouse. The 2066 voyage of the *Alexandrian*, financed and filmed by Al Jazeera, made "Ben-dere" and her crew international celebs.

APRIL 8, 2523. Gautama Door debut. World's third-largest engineering project is dedicated on the Buddha's 2,000th birthday. SinoIndia hopes that the 90-kilometer-wide cut in the Himalayas will open the Tibetan plateau to monsoon moisture and stimulate stratorice production.

APRIL 13, 2077. Mex-Can gets max. After a contentious 120-gigabyte hearing, the convicted serial hacker (aka Julio Pugh Jr.) is sentenced to life offline without parole. It is the Web-Watcher AI's most severe penalty to date.

APRIL 29, 2056. Moplicans™ shine. Declaring an early end to Oilspill Emma, BP president Chloe Washburn credits Biodubon's new gen-altered pelicans, which can soak up as much as 110 times their weight in crude before they are recalled and crushed.

MAY 6, 2029. Spiderman turned off. Broadway's third-longest-running hit, *Spiderman: Turn Off the Dark*, closes without opening after 18 years of sell-out rehearsals. Controversial new union rules restricting fatalities to one per week blamed.

MAY 14, 2114. Locusts eat Taj Mahal. Christian terrorists suspected in reintroduction of forbidden entomological bioweaponry, banned since the Plague War.

MAY 22, 2039. Jobs buys British Columbia. The land grant from the patriotic octogenarian megabillionaire connects Alaska with the lower 48.

MAY 26, 2076. Solar storm blanks banks. The sudden collapse of the electronic currency system leads to new calls for the restoration of paper money.

JUNE 4, 2154. Sandhill cranes sighted. Orniphiles gather to gawk at mating pair discovered in suburban Lagos. The once-numerous migratory birds have been feared extinct since the global magnetic field reversal in 2139.

JUNE 11, 2109. Horse takes Triple Crown. The 2:07 Belmont Stakes win for long shot Son of Sam has handicappers predicting that thoroughbreds will return to the Sport of Kings, dominated by six-legged proprietary biobreds since the early years of the century.

JUNE 14, 2051. Philadelphia freaks. Four killed, 11 injured as riots erupt downtown during UNIVAC I centennial ceremony. Bad birthday cake blamed.

JUNE 27, 2066. Frack hits Canaries. Damage light at 4.9 RS. The mobile exploratory tremor, originally licensed to Long Island Gas, has been oscillating undersea since going rogue in 2049, apparently feeding on rotational stress.

JULY 1, 2062. Lincoln deleted from Rushmore. Fulfilling a campaign promise, President Paul personally dynamites the face of the tax-and-spender who established the income tax and the IRS on this date in 1862. Lincoln's image will be replaced by that of Paul's grandfather.

JULY 19, 2123. Lunar battlefield dedicated. In a solemn vid ceremony viewed by millions, 12 volunteers are executed at Mare Tracy to commemorate the dozen who died in the opening skirmish of the Helium Wars.

JULY 11, 2176. Mao leaves Memphis. Grateful locals wave farewell as *The Chairman* heads home. The Chinese nuclear sub has provided the Upper South with power since the New New Madrid quake in 2169.

JULY 23, 2104. "Clocker" Wheeler dies. The inventor of the controlled clockwise countertornado is credited with saving St. Louis in 2077.

AUGUST 3, 2076. New Veterans Day. Invoking her powers as commander-in-chief, President Junni inducts 228 million draftees into the National Guard. Their honorable discharge in 24 hours will guarantee medical care for all Americans through the Veterans Administration.

AUGUST 9, 2032. K2 falls to ATV. Brunei sportsman Abu Wadi summits the world's second-highest mountain in a 599 cc Kawasaki Sherpa. The 8,600-meter Himalayan peak is the highest yet conquered by an all-terrain vehicle.

AUGUST 13, 2233. Comet ignites. Harley-Wu 4 ("Lady Kerosene") lights up the heavens for a two-week solar transit, inspiring poets and prospectors as the Oort cloud oil rush gets underway.

AUGUST 23, 2112. Yellow grass tops Donner Pass. Alarmed biologists fear that the mutant graminoid, which has been spreading west from Yucca Mountain since the repository was reopened in April, will cover the Central Valley within a year.

SEPTEMBER 2, 2105. *Harvest Moon* sinks. The luxury cruiser for volunteer organ donors is lost in a storm off Lagos, triggering a crash in the health-care commodities market.

SEPTEMBER 12, 2025. Writers riot. An estimated 75,000 unemployed creative writing instructors trash downtown Iowa City in the most violent literary protest since the collapse of the MFA bubble in 2019.

SEPTEMBER 14, 2113. Saska dies. The world's largest single organism, the beloved 2,925-square-kilometer bitumirhizome uncovered in the Canadian oil sands, officially expires at 9:04 p.m. CST. Global warming blamed.

SEPTEMBER 18, 2034. Dead heat at Emmys. In a rare split decision, Fox's popular suicide series, *American Ashes*, shares top reality TV honors with ABC's teen-oriented *Kevorkers*. Both producers, urns in arms, praised participants.

OCTOBER 4, 2116. Finns take Stornoway. The predawn parasail assault begins the war for control of Scotland's kelp plantations, source of 67% of the world's biofuel energy.

OCTOBER 10, 2165. No shorts, no service. US Parks Department adopts controversial dress code requiring pants for Skeeters™. The short-lived hairless flash clones, which have no digestive or reproductive systems, are popular with campers, who deploy them to draw away insect pests.

OCTOBER 11, 2045. Show-Me IPO. Shares in Missouri Christian (formerly Missouri) soar with rumors that the first fully privatized state will allow nonvested residents to purchase voting and free-speech rights.

OCTOBER 21, 2106. Oldest human hits 200. Birthday greetings pour into North Plainfield as marathon ager Nanci Funt begins her third century. The diminutive organ-tank vet woke briefly to wave thanks to sponsors Blisterex™, Kaiser Health Sales and *Liquid Life* magazine.

NOVEMBER 3, 2023. Dallas wedding panic. Mixed-sex marriages suspended with discovery that 11,244 locals, ages 19 to 31, are descended from a single donor, the CEO of budget sperm bank Christian Dad. Gown, tux and cake sales sink.

NOVEMBER 10, 2176. Doc Chosmey dies. The Nigerian linguist is credited with inventing Muse™, the popular mail-order language neither written nor spoken but used for introspection only. Muse™ thinkers worldwide are estimated at 4.5 billion.

NOVEMBER 14, 2215. Galactic leader stoned. Bubba Li, the controversial day boss of the Galactic Disciples, captured in his third attempt to retake Cleveland, is executed by teens in a public ceremony.

NOVEMBER 19, 2055. Blue laws outlawed. In a 5–4 decision, US Supreme Court strikes down state and local restrictions on Sunday liquor sales, declaring them versions of Sharia law, prohibited by the 28th Amendment to the Constitution.

DECEMBER 8, 1980. Lennon lives. A wild shot by a deranged fan allows the rock star time to write his Tony-winning *Quantum Opera* and gives rise to the alternate universe from which this item was posted.

DECEMBER 11, 2184. Asteroid misses Earth. Pakistani jihadinauts blamed for near-fatal approach of NEO yu57. Secret solar sail array was used to facilitate planetary suicide attempt.

DECEMBER 19, 2038. Wall Street raid. Some 44 illicit day traders, seven of them women, are arrested in biggest Fed-NYPD operation since equity speculation was restricted to alternate Mondays under Sylciby-Grant. Alleged police brutality under investigation by ACLU.

DECEMBER 25, 2104. Mormons win Yule 500. After a dramatic last-lap pass of Scientology's Kia, the checkered flag goes to the benzine-powered LDS Stude. It's the Christian spin-off's first undisputed win in the annual UNASCAR event open to all the world's religions.

2012

JANUARY 1, 2033. Grand Canyon Drive opens. The result of a historic compromise with environmentalists, the scenic riverside parkway is invisible from rim viewpoints and accessible only to electric and hybrid vehicles.

JANUARY 4, 2254. It's c steady! The speed of light, slowing since 2011, stabilizes at 299,792,341 meters per second. Physicists anticipate a gradual return to the traditional 299,792,458 mps, speculating speed bumps in the space-time continuum.

JANUARY 10, 2104. "Happy" Holiday dies. The maverick millionaire endocrinologist synthesized and marketed the *Sciuridae* (squirrel) hormone Startenstop™ so popular with dancers, shy teens and the military.

JANUARY 28, 2019. Fog closes Congress. Recess declared as the sulphurous cloud seeping from the Harrisburg Slump reaches DC, prompting new calls to regulate fracking.

FEBRUARY 4, 2054. Good behavior. Faithful rejoice as Pope Gregory-Yang is released after serving only six months of his 12-year sentence as an accessory to child abuse.

FEBRUARY 11, 2107. Cochin Cola closes Greenland ice cap. Commodity markets surge as tap futures top out at €110 a barrel, a 12-month high.

FEBRUARY 12, 2015. Occupy Keystone incorporates. The population-55,000 (est.) tent city in the Nebraska sandhills, the largest in the 99%'s nationwide network, is the first to be awarded a zip code.

FEBRUARY 24, 2112. SeaWorld© buys Bagram. The former US air base and detention center is scheduled to reopen May 1 with enhanced torture exhibits rivaling Cuba's popular Guantanamo theme park.

MARCH 4, 2032. Downer disappears. The cross-platform rogue avatar led the wargames shooter mutiny, demanding resurrection pay for combat toons. Foul play suspected.

MARCH 6, 2066. Oscar gets Oscar. It is the first time the Academy has awarded Best Picture honors to a 3D documentary, to a film shown only at the awards ceremony and to a film about itself. Anita Spielberg-Cameron accepts.

MARCH 14, 2188. Einstein birthday. His theory of relativity, retropatented by Federal Express in 2116, led to a revolution in—and redefinition of—on-time delivery. That's his face on the sails of the FedEx brigantines.

MARCH 11, 2105. Let 'em eat caveyar. Riots erupt in Hannipitowne, Sicily's largest refugee camp, protesting new protein-rich diet. The fish egg paste, now farmed worldwide, was once considered a luxury.

APRIL 5, 2044. Beverly Hills quarantined. Cholera epidemic is traced to the popularity of internal cosmetic surgery, which replaces the customary odor of fecal material with proprietary scents such as English Spring™ and Sea Breeze™.

APRIL 1, 2021. Antidiscrimination victory. President Lee signs bill outlawing consideration of race in college applications. Also prohibited are considerations of gender, age, athletic ability, sexual orientation, grades, test scores, geographic origin and alumnal connection.

FEBRUARY 22, 2201. Nile runs. In what is seen as a hopeful sign for the new century, the once-mighty river flows into the Mediterranean for the first time since 2116.

MARCH 28, 2092. Sideman "dies." The beloved robot arbiter was famous for negotiating an end to the bloody 12-year trade war that began in 2078 when an Amazon price drone was shot down inside Philadelphia's Liberty Mall.

MAY 6, 2031. Tenner topples Tokyo. Massive hour-long quake kills 2.6 million and calls into question the use of preemptive fracking to ease tension on thrust faults.

MAY 13, 2061. Faye bids farewell. America's first transgender president resigns under protest to avoid impeachment vote after felony conviction for smoking within 1,200 meters of an elementary school. She claims entrapment since her cigarette was lit by a Secret Service volunteer.

MAY 22, 2109. Buffalo Bill shot. The popular genetically modified bison, which recited the Lord's Prayer over and over in low tones, is shot while on a tour of state capitols by a disgruntled NRA atheist.

MAY 26, 2115. Italy awarded *Adriatic Queen*. The International Maritime Court decision ends a 44-year legal battle over salvage rights to the sunken cruise liner, which is worth an estimated €450,000 in artificial hips and knees.

JUNE 4, 2143. Petrodads swarm Gulf oil rig. All hands lost. The 6-foot semiorganic silicon crayfish, bioengineered to feed on oil slicks, have reproduced in record numbers since going rogue during the 2126 *Exxon Titanic* disaster. Coast Guard plans inquiry.

JUNE 8, 2098. "Yo ho, H_2O." Using sled dogs and ski planes, Somali pirates seize Pepsico's 25,000-ton Antarctic berg as it is being towed into the Arabian Sea en route to New Dubai. The freshwater slab is valued at CN¥1.1 million.

JUNE 14, 2451. UNIVAC's 500th. Droll reenactors in period lab coats festooned with magnetic tape delight Philadelphians as they boot up a replica of UNIVAC I, born on this day in 1951.

JUNE 19, 2046. First Freedom Plaza dedicated. Springsteen sings "Born in the U.S.A." as the 12-acre site in Northwestern Oklahoma is officially declared open to all documented US citizens who wish to exercise their First Amendment rights. Overnight camping banned.

JULY 2, 2101. Bette Lo dies. The celebrated Puerto Rican game designer won the 2063 digital Pulitzer for her holographic 3D RPG Tarantulaba, which reverses Alzheimer's in players. She was 107.

JULY 13, 2176. Harvard book burning. Suicide students protesting ATMs that prepay (deduct) edu-loan interest from withdrawals torch themselves inside the online Ivy's 112-story Phoenix campus library.

JULY 21, 2041. Final gorilla interred. Millions mourn via satlink as Rudyard, the last of the mountain *berengei*, is buried in Westminster Abbey. Ransomed from poachers, the body was flown in state from Rwanda in exchange for Commonwealth status.

JULY 23, 2076. World's worst air disaster. All 1,219 aboard lost as TrampAir's popular Glasgow-Dubai standing-room-only flight 11 is shot down by a rogue NATO drone over Cyprus. Evasion software malfunction suspected.

AUGUST 9, 2022. Manhattan eat-in. Union Square closed as angry obies block streets and doorways protesting new BMI-30 law fining restaurants that seat or serve persons who appear overweight. They are also not allowed to buy potato chips.

AUGUST 11, 2104. Arch assault. Eleven natural bridges in Utah, Kentucky and Arizona brought down by simultaneous blasts. Mundanes claim responsibility as part of their campaign against natural wonders, which began with Niagara.

AUGUST 17, 2149. Antarctic gold rush. Defying a Goldman-NATO blockade and sub-subzero temps, the *Caribbean Princess* lands 1,800 queenies, the first to hit the ice since twitters of a heavy metal meteor breaking up over Queen Anne Land went viral in May. Millions will follow.

AUGUST 21, 2023. VW buys Greek Isles. Euro stocks soar in an apparent thumbs-up to the German automaker's bid to expand into travel and tourism.

SEPTEMBER 3, 2027. Whale call victory. Overruling previous bans, International Oceanic Council approves Kia-Aquatic's subsonar echolator, which gathers whales for slaughter with a "call-to-prayer" click array. Free speech concerns cited.

SEPTEMBER 12, 2108. Wright stuff. The 200th anniversary of the first fatal air crash is celebrated in Virginia by two suicide reenactors in a replica Wright brothers biplane for an appreciative crowd of 124 aviation buffs.

SEPTEMBER 19, 2032. Aaaargh! Talk Like a Pirate Day cancelled by FCC in anticipation of "toxic flood" of homophobic, racist, sexist, bullying and abusive language on AM talk radio.

SEPTEMBER 25, 2065. First 4D movie. Record billion-dollar opening for TikTok Entertainment's *Spidergirl: Third Date*. Industry analysts credit chronoflex technology enabling moviegoers to experience feature-length films in 8–10 minutes.

OCTOBER 3, 2057. *Polynya Princess* "tops out." Beating rival Disney's *Arctic Deb* by less than one hour, the 4,400-passenger Celebrity liner is the first cruise ship to reach the North Pole. All patio-class passengers get a 90-day tattoo.

OCTOBER 12, 2074. Mars attack. Exploratory Martius Minerals rover caravan ambushed in Mare Silenius by Chinese drones armed with phosphorus bombs. Historians consider the Mare Massacre the first off-planet robotic industrial war crime.

OCTOBER 14, 2286. Stonehenge discovered. The famed prehistoric monument, missing since 2279, is found by a cleaning lady in the chapel of a Salt Lake City community college. Buckingham Palace demands return, apology.

OCTOBER 26, 2165. Herman "Merman" Moore dies. The Ohio-born jurist was the first Supreme Court justice with a jellyfish heart, now required in all federal appellate court appointees.

NOVEMBER 4, 2076. Verizon for veep. Randolph-Verizon Republican presidential victory marks first national elective office won by a corporation since the ratification of the Personhood Amendment (the nation's 29th) in 2054.

NOVEMBER 14, 2166. Lake licks Loop. Chicago mayor Dayly declares Aquaday as Lake Michigan officially reaches 20th-century level. The freshwater inland sea was accidentally drained by a downstate fracking error in 2098.

NOVEMBER 22, 2041. China buys student debt. Grateful US indentured grads offered liability release via two-year community service enlistment in Chinese childcare and soft coal extraction brigades.

NOVEMBER 28, 2102. Chez Sauterelle opens. The *trés chic* Berkeley eatery is credited with helping to end the nation's dependence on corn-fed meat with its fashionable *cuisine croquant* featuring organic protein from the Nebraska free-range locust ranches.

DECEMBER 3, 2114. *Hoover* hit. UNASA's celebrated cleanup satellite is struck by a meteor, scattering debris that will brighten night skies and down airliners for decades to come.

DECEMBER 11, 2313. Paradise found. Surprising scientists, scholars and Christians alike, the actual biblical heaven, filled with immortal blessed souls, is discovered in the Oort cloud by a prospector drone. It's tiny.

DECEMBER 19, 2019. Last call. Road rage rules in nationwide run on liquor stores as distilleries pull stock, protesting new FDA rule requiring graphic DUI victim images on bottles. Reported 766 deaths in Cincinnati alone.

DECEMBER 24, 2040. Prophets Day. Responding to Ecumenical Retail Council request, Congress declares the last Monday in December a federal holiday celebrating the births of Joseph Smith, Jesus Christ and Isaac Newton.

2013

JANUARY 1, 2077. Elixir Order. In a bipartisan congressional effort to save Social Security, the legal age of all Americans born in 2007 is reduced by ten years. The 4.3 million citizens affected are compensated with free dental care and a $1,200 Amazon gift card.

JANUARY 3, 2091. Airliner clips cloud. Financial markets tremble as NY–LA Delta jet wings and scatters the ultralite ununoctium striated Cirrus databank backing up the world's infocurrency. GPS error blamed.

JANUARY 14, 2105. Airbag attack. Estimated 6,500 killed in rush hour chaos as Missouri drone triggers Indiana airbags in major escalation of the War between the States.

JANUARY 23, 2321. *Curiosity* found. The twisted remains of the lost 21st-century robot explorer are discovered by trekkers under the southwestern scarp of Olympus Mons. The rover, which went rogue in 2019, was apparently trying to summit the solar system's highest peak when it fell.

FEBRUARY 4, 2065. Franchise fix. Responding to a contentious, decade-long "No Representation without Taxation" campaign, Congress restricts federal voting rights to employed persons between the ages of 20 and 65. AARP protests coup.

FEBRUARY 11, 2321. Zodiac switch. The sudden 164-degree shift in star maps, at 6:56 a.m. MT (Mecca Time), is attributed to a change in galactic orientation of the solar system, perhaps caused by a space-time fold. Astrologers scramble to rewrite planetaries.

FEBRUARY 19, 2025. NCAA settles. All college football players who dressed for a bowl game since 1968 to get $1 million tax-free. Eleven college presidents on suicide watch as NAACP, which initiated lawsuit, promises further attacks on "student slavery."

FEBRUARY 24, 2176. Mars or bust. SpaceX offers one-way cold sleep steerage to fourth planet, tidally locked by a series of controlled-fusion pulses. The new Earth-like climate on the sunlit half of the Red Planet is expected to draw millions of "daytimers."

MARCH 2, 2021. Jobs hosts Oscars. In a Hollywood holographic first, the late Apple CEO hosts the 93rd Academy Awards to mixed reviews. iCar sales soar.

MARCH 6, 2036. Alone Star State. Texas denied reentry into USA. House rejects repatriation petition in 435–0 roll call vote hailed as "second Alamo" by Vice President Rivera-Goldberg.

MARCH 12, 2104. Cologne Cathedral falls. Once the tallest building in the world, the medieval landmark is brought down by a single suitcase bomb, thought to be in response to a papal cartoon lampooning Scientology.

MARCH 23, 2087. Boot gets boot. Supreme Court bans Arizona's 40-pound penalty shoe for student loan scofflaws, declaring it "cruel if not unusual."

APRIL 1, 2020. Romney does a Richard. The body of the presidential candidate, missing since late 2012, is discovered in a stalled car elevator in California. Tests to determine if he's alive or not are inconclusive.

APRIL 4, 2113. Drone attack. Chicago's entire fleet of 344 surveillance drones is destroyed by suicide pigeons. Gang activity suspected.

APRIL 6, 2031. Robeson Hall. The legendary NYC concert venue formerly known as Carnegie Hall is renamed in honor of the once-blacklisted singer and civil rights hero, born on this day in 1898. Pete Seeger hosts ceremony.

APRIL 13, 2029. Celestial slap. The stadium-size asteroid Apophis skips off Earth's upper atmosphere, creating a shock wave that downs two 787s and a container zep. Asteroid Watch promises software update.

MAY 1, 2020. Mayday! In the first intercontinental general strike, Mujeres Unidas shuts down an estimated 90% of shops, schools, hotels, factories and websites in North and South America. The union, which formed in 2016 as a Walmart associates caucus, demands universal health care and child care.

MAY 9–11, 2107. Ceticide. The entire global population of the planet's largest animal, 3,912 blue whales (*Balaenoptera musculus*), beach themselves and die on Long Island's south shore in an apparent mass suicide.

MAY 19, 2024. Reparations. In partial compensation for the forced labor and lost wealth of slavery, African Americans over the age of 18 are permitted to smoke anywhere they want. Except New York City.

MAY 21, 2044. Squatters' rights. In a close roll call vote overriding a Security Council veto, the UN recognizes Detroit as an urban free state. Formerly part of the USA, the city was seized by an army of *sin*-docs in 2037.

JUNE 8, 2125. Sister Nonamous dies. The hacker nun who posted 1,857 proprietary pharmaceutical formulas on the Internet in 2078 was serving a life sentence for industrial espionage; she is survived, according to Father Joe Celia, her confessor, "by the million souls she saved."

JUNE 19, 2053. Prize for spies. On the 100th anniversary of their execution for espionage, Julius and Ethel Rosenberg receive the Chomsky Peace Prize for their role in making it impossible for the United States to use nuclear weapons in Korea and Vietnam.

JUNE 22, 2111. Tartan-in-Thames. London under health watch as dead salmon choke the Thames as far as Westminster. The colorful GMO Black Watch–plaid suicide fish, which die instead of spawn, were released to protest England's repo of Scotland after the 2109 bankruptcy.

JUNE 24, 2055. *Dora* steps out. After a nail-biter touchdown, with a jaunty wave to the folks back home, UNASA's newest Mars rover strolls off to explore the Red Planet. The solar-powered bipedal humanoid robot is designed to stimulate public interest in extraplanetary research.

JULY 4, 2022. Flash mob says "Good Morning America." Tourists drop signs and flee as 1,400 college students overwhelm ABC security and unroll banners demanding debt relief.

JULY 11, 2029. Drone takes Talladega. Angry fans trash stands, burn checkered flags as Penske's remote-controlled Honda wins NASCAR's 300-mile Southern Sprint.

JULY 12, 2054. Alaska Purchase. Russian bittionaire Zavyd Imogydiski buys northernmost US state for ฿17.9 billion (ADJ), in what is hailed as the world's largest single Bitcoin transaction.

JULY 23, 2116. Carnival's *Comfort Queen* seized in war crimes investigation. The hospice cruise liner is suspected to be a recruitment vehicle for suicide bombers. Lawyers without Borders promises appeal.

AUGUST 5, 2059. Google completes photo imaging of ocean floor. The online clipart archive was once a major international corporation.

AUGUST 11, 2106. Trebek retires. Millions mourn as the robotic game show host is disassembled after a 122-year run on *Jeopardy*. His popularity soared after his true identity was revealed in a 2054 paternity suit.

AUGUST 21, 2066. MacMeat goes organic. Sales of America's bestselling in vitro beef burger triple after FDA certifies that the only artificial ingredient is the product itself.

AUGUST 24, 2104. Unicorn gores girls. Twelve die in Pasadena Princess Parade rampage, leading to new calls for restrictions on GMO fantasy animals.

SEPTEMBER 4, 2165. Leprosy saved. Hansen's bacterium, or *M. leprae*, is taken off the UN's endangered disease list as 221 volunteers are certified infected. The new carriers, all members of We Are Habitat, will be quarantined in an Armadillo, Oklahoma, leprosarium.

SEPTEMBER 17, 2104. Twister goes rogue. EcoJersey's stationary weather structure slips grid, dimming lights from Hartford, Connecticut, to DC, and has to be put down by federal Power Rangers after demolishing Princeton's adjunct dorm. The dead include four PhDs.

SEPTEMBER 23, 2091. Fireworks on Mars. The 19-minute display, visible from Earth, raises new hopes of contact with the so-called Lost Colony. It is thought to be a centennial display since the Christian settlement at New Ararat traces its origin to Armenian Independence in 1991.

SEPTEMBER 26, 2043. First woman in NBA. Accompanied by her agent and NBA president Dimita Storm, Mary Lou Flynn reports to Los Angeles Lakers training camp with game face on. Before her dramatic postseason gender-affirming surgery, the Lakers' star forward led the league in assists as Michael Louis Flynn.

OCTOBER 2, 2027. Bloody Monday. Shoot-out in New Jersey mall leaves 77 dead, prompting demands for 8 p.m. senior curfew to curb escalating violence between "geezer gangs." ACLU warns against profiling.

OCTOBER 11, 2044. Get out of college free. Howard University Students for a Free Society issues national call to repudiate student debt. Millions respond by flooding banks with Monopoly™ money.

OCTOBER 24, 2045. Climate cops. UN centenary celebrated by formation of Global Commons Authority, a new international agency regulating all activities affecting seas and atmosphere.

OCTOBER 26, 2031. Channel crossing X'd. The first underwater English Channel swim is declared void after former Olympic champ Brenda Bleriotte tests positive for myoglobin, found in whale and seal blood. Vampirism and animal abuse charges pending.

NOVEMBER 9, 2044. Bad dad busted. Oscar Lee of Berkeley, California, is fined 400 media minutes for allowing his 6-year-old son, Dale, to ride his tricycle without a helmet. The kid's OK.

NOVEMBER 15, 2025. Ms. Conduct. Fulfilling her most controversial campaign promise, President Warren signs "Fair Play" bill requiring prosecutors to serve out terms of wrongly convicted prisoners. American Bar Association threatens hunger strike.

NOVEMBER 21, 2134. Gabby Guerin shot. The celebrity inventor of Happitalk™, the synthetic intestinal flora that enhances language acquisition, is assassinated by unemployed ESL instructor, who then kills herself with a bicycle lock.

NOVEMBER 23, 2103. Russian rescue. Longshoremen cheer as the container ship *China Dollar* enters Baltimore harbor, closed since 2099 by a massive jellyfish bloom. Russia's nuclear icebreaker *Ubey Seksista* opened the channel. Norfolk next.

DECEMBER 4, 2025. Rok'em reined in. The North Korean boy band, whose cover of the Cher megahit "Bang Bang" is credited with over 154 teen murders, is banned from pod play in Boston, Riyadh and Berkeley.

DECEMBER 7, 2105. Drone center down. After LAX near-disaster, FAA grounds Skycap of Omaha, nation's largest contract flyer, pending inquiry; meanwhile, onboard pilots "strongly suggested" for interstate flights.

DECEMBER 10, 2051. Dewey Debris™ debut. UNASA's new safety system launched on 200th birthday of librarian-inventor Melvil Dewey. No longer needed for books, Dewey's 1886 decimal system has been updated to a positional avoidance grid for orbital trash.

DECEMBER 24, 2076. Happy holidays. Scholars celebrate as Ed-Sec Patricia Sweany raises grad bonus from $500 to $1,000. First major educational reform since high school students won health care and $125 weekly stipend in 2066.

2014

JANUARY 7, 2017. "*Here's Chelsea!*" A record 100 million viewers (Nielsen rating 77.4) tune in to the afternoon talk show hosted by Nobel Peace Prize laureate Chelsea Manning. Manning signed with OWN TV shortly after her release was ordered by the International War Crimes Tribunal.

JANUARY 11, 2132. My Moai! Ownership of the 22 Easter Island–like statues discovered by lunar ³H prospectors in Mare Ingenii is awarded to United Pacific States. Chile plans protest.

JANUARY 22, 2054. Billy Gaga buys MIR-9. The diminutive Hollywood mogul plans to refit the aging orbital station for special effects work.

JANUARY 26, 2106. Thank you for your service. Baffin Air's flagship DC-3 lands at Orange County Air Museum, ending the longest run of any production airliner design.

FEBRUARY 14, 2133. Reverse marriage approved. The tight (.53–.47) assembly vote follows an intense four-year campaign in which the institution was described variously as a "geezer grinder" and a "reverse mortgage with love instead of money."

FEBRUARY 11, 2019. Papa Rizzo killed in crash. For a $1,200 fee he would involve clients in personal auto accidents with Hollywood stars. He always rode along.

FEBRUARY 19, 2032. First manned Mars landing. Sporting Kickstarter T-shirts over space tights, the *Endeavour II* crew debarks at Eberswalde Crater rim, gamely smiling for the web despite the news that their return voyage is only 11% funded.

FEBRUARY 21, 2255. Close call. ErthGaard's first test of its new time gun prompts loud huzzahs as a deadly asteroid threatening Cozumel is sent back 65 million years.

MARCH 1, 2022. Call on the wild. Eastern (aka Timber) wolves (*Canis lupus lycaon*) reintroduced to Detroit suburbs to cull deer and discourage squatters.

MARCH 16, 2021. Gun control. Heralding a "new era of safety," President Warren signs "Heads Up" bill requiring concealed-carry permit holders to fire a warning shot before entering schools, bars and theaters. Protestant churches exempted.

MARCH 22, 2122. Apple introduces 4D printer. Whatever you make, you already have a copy of. And it won't print ugly stuff.

MARCH 26, 2067. March Madness. Flash mob of supporters fills court at Duke-UK game as players sit down demanding minimum wage, health care and an end to literacy tests for varsity seniors.

APRIL 1®, 2037. April Fool®. April 1st, often celebrated with pranks and hoaxes, is bought by Comedy Central for an undisclosed 11-figure sum. First major commons acquisition since Marvel's surprise purchase of Christmas Eve®.

APRIL 9, 2143. Ride 'em cowboy. Film fans pack plexes as 11,322 Westerns are simultaneously rereleased, digitally scrubbed of cigarettes and guns in accordance with Cinema Code 1121.

APRIL 19, 2099. Direct elections okayed. President Nuñez signs voter relief bill allowing congressional races to be decided by simple count of campaign dollars raised. Dems and Teas alike praise electoral streamlining.

APRIL 22, 2176. Synthisect swarm. Thousands flee in terror as the locust-size biodevices munch a bloody mile-wide path through Chicago suburbs. Introduced by Monsanto to destroy off-license soybeans, the colorful proprietary bugs have recently developed a taste for small dogs and children.

MAY 3, 2054. DC drone attack. Nasal nanodrones disrupt cabinet meeting and injure four, including Vice President Rubio-

Steiner, treated at Hillary General for nosebleed. Congress calls for new White House screens.

MAY 19, 2061. Zapped. Fatal coronaries fell 112 people in Los Angeles when an unruly antiprivatization protest is fog-tazed outside AARP's Sunset hospice prison. LAPD promises review of crowd-control tech.

MAY 22, 2165. Leno doc honored. Madge Ryder, MD, whose distinctive squirrel brain chinplants have given new life to thousands of stroke victims, receives the AMA's coveted Surgery Cup in a celebrity-studded Denver food court ceremony at age 99.

MAY 29, 2104. United 333 found. The Lagos-bound Boeing 820 superliner, which mysteriously disappeared May 11, is found in low Earth orbit with all 455 passengers and crew declared recoverable deceased. Sudden malfunction of GE's new hydrogen plasma engines suspected.

JUNE 2, 2113. Mountaintop retrieval. In a historic EPA settlement, Peabody Coal agrees to restore Kentucky's Black Mountain to its original 4,150-foot elevation, with an added 3,500-foot penalty. The resulting 7,650-foot peak will be the tallest in the eastern United States.

JUNE 14, 2051. Joy to the World. Laptops, pads and cell phones worldwide play overture to Handel's *Messiah* to celebrate 100th birthday of UNIVAC I.

JUNE 19, 2065. Drink up! For the first time since the 2049 Keystone disaster, the Ogallala Aquifer is declared potable for adults and animals. High Plains tap still unsafe for seniors and infants.

JUNE 22, 2034. Drone docks. After an uneventful 40-day voyage, the *China Dutchman* is eased into Long Beach Harbor by an onboard union pilot. The first container ship to cross the Pacific without a crew, the 55,000-ton vessel is powered by a mix of sail and solar steam.

JULY 3, 2105. Cerulean survival. Polar bears (*Ursus maritimus*) removed from endangered list as Extinction Alert confirms 74% born dark blue with flippers. Swift adaptation to loss of sea ice prompts new research into evolutionary triggers.

JULY 12, 2076. Two riders approaching. Alice Fedler's bestselling novelization of Bob Dylan's "All Along the Watchtower" wins coveted PEN/Prosation prize. First win by female author since Kate Proon's 266-page *Dover Beach* in 2061.

JULY 16, 2031. Indigents chipped. Los Angeles homeless fitted with intradermal GPS to expedite monitoring by social workers. A low-intensity shock discourages clients from leaving their service area.

JULY 26, 2044. Poltroon's revenge. Afternoon talk show host Calvin Mays killed in black-powder 10-pacer by insulted Indiana governor Dermont Hood. First televised duel since affairs of honor declared free speech by Supreme Court in 2039.

AUGUST 2, 2055. Luxury liner. Brunei Air inaugurates new Sharia 777 service. Men fly first and business class; women in coach.

AUGUST 11, 2104. March on Washington. Protesting new Educational Opportunity Administration, which replaces selective college admissions with national lottery, rampaging Ivy alumni overturn 12 trash cans. Four arrests.

AUGUST 20, 2113. New New Madrid quake. Eleven-pointer topples Memphis Memorial Tower, straightens the Mississippi River and kills an estimated 210,000 people, including Chevron Danceathon host Aristide Glum.

AUGUST 28, 2088. Shoppers' fallen star. Charlotte's MVP center Harriet "Bruce" Wayne is killed in a skydiving accident. Bought (and renamed) by IKEA in 2079, the Charlotte Shoppers are the first all-gay NBA team and the first to have a female starter.

SEPTEMBER 9, 2022. Children threaten America. Taserfog and semilethal toy bullets turn back illegal-alien orphan army marching on Washington seeking education, health care and security. President praises Health, Education and Welfare for tough-love tactics.

SEPTEMBER 11, 2101. No thanks. Flying low, loud and fast, US protest drones disrupt Islamic Caliphate ceremony celebrating 9/11 martyrs centennial. Eleven of 19 suicide re-enactors fail to die.

SEPTEMBER 20, 2106. Anni Awards brawl. An estimated 1.4 billion worldwide watch in horror as Tommy Turtle is chopped into pieces on the red carpet by Paula Bunyan. Nominated Best Character for her role in Pixicar's 4D hit *Axe Lady*, she wore a denim gown by L.L.L.Bean and a meat mask.

SEPTEMBER 22, 2077. Online ossuary. Realtors rejoice as Arlington National Cemetery is replaced by an ad-free FB page. The 624 acres will be subdivided for luxury housing and eco-friendly mini-malls.

OCTOBER 3, 2026. Heathrow revolt. King Charles calls for calm as thousands of quarantined travelers storm through exit barricades and stream into London. The airport, once Europe's busiest, has been on lockdown for 22 days in an effort to slow the spread of the 3bola variant.

OCTOBER 19, 2077. Irish artist and Nobel Peace Prize laureate Paula Fitzhill dies in Dublin. Her dramatic black-and-white *Gaza*, based on Picasso's *Guernica*, now hangs in the atrium of the United Nations in Jerusalem.

OCTOBER 28, 2086. Ms. Liberty recall. Silent, surly Tricolor Temps dismantle and crate the statue that once welcomed "your tired, your poor, your huddled masses" to New York Harbor. It will be returned to Paris by air.

OCTOBER 29, 2112. Triple disaster. The sudden reversal of the Earth's geomagnetic field turns tragic as three Aeroflot 797s are downed, one by ball lightning and two by a mile-high mass of confused migratory birds.

NOVEMBER 11, 2087. Rogue cops captured. Athens Police Department in Ohio surrenders to federal Bureau of Alcohol, Firearms, Tobacco and Explosives in Lyton, Kentucky. The heavily armed police department took over the Kentucky town in September after being driven from Ohio by angry residents.

NOVEMBER 14, 2254. Pioneering neurosurgeon dies. Dr. Carla Levin's patented nanolaser needle file made possible the burgeoning science of cosmetic brain surgery. She was 28.

NOVEMBER 24, 2159. Book burning. Convicted creationist hacker Commander Cain denies involvement as all digital copies of Darwin's *On the Origin of Species* disappear on the bicentennial of its 1859 publication.

NOVEMBER 28, 2365. Rum day. Hundreds of pirate-garbed partiers drown as freak autumn storm swamps pontoon ship *Jolly Roger* during Hudson Bay Regatta. Global warming, alcohol blamed.

DECEMBER 2, 2044. Halley's beheaded. Continuing its jihad against "unholy images," the Caliphate shoots down the celebrated comet on its periodic appearance. Struck by a laser beam from Baghdad, the shooting star's coma (or head) is detached from the tail and falls into the sun. It was apparently thought to be man-made.

DECEMBER 13, 2052. Hackers hit and run. Cloudcoding "suicide Chevys" and "crazy Camrys" to plow into storefronts, run down pedestrians and snarl traffic, Anonymous avenges Fed's Bitcoin devaluation. Google sends regrets.

DECEMBER 16, 2108. Brooklyn downsizes. AmericanMayor stock soars as the iconic borough secedes from New York City in order to adopt AM's popular RFD.02 (Mayberry) municipal software package, guaranteeing employment, housing and health care for all.

DECEMBER 24, 2347. Sorcerers Day. Celebrations of the birth of the transistor in Bell Labs, New Jersey, and of J. Christ in Bethlehem, Palestine, are combined into one interplanetary holiday.

2015

JANUARY 3, 2076. Spinning Stetson. Tulsa's iconic Cowboy Hat revolving restaurant hurls diners, waiters and tableware off 80-story skyscraper. The 333 rpm 77-second spin, blamed on a windfarm electrical surge, kills 86, including Tulsa's part-time mayor, W. "Woe" Wilson, who was working as maître d'.

JANUARY 14, 2105. Labor victory! Congress approves mandatory 28-hour work week. Freelance writers exempted.

JANUARY 22, 2154. Dogs outlawed. Protest leashes pile up outside CDC as canine sequestration begins. The "petting death" will claim another 1.5 million victims before the nolovirus and its host, *Canis lupus familiaris*, are officially extincted in 2159.

JANUARY 28, 2033. Amelia Streach born in Fountain, Nebraska. Elected in 2072 as Allen Streach, he was the first transgender president and the first sitting US president to orbit Earth.

FEBRUARY 6, 2154. Music City zapped. Downtown Nashville leveled by four-day lightning swarm visible from as far away as St. Louis. Scientists blame increased atmospheric electrical activity on leakage from Arizona solar arrays.

FEBRUARY 11, 2129. Apostolic repossession. Granted independence by Mussolini in 1929, Vatican City is reclaimed by Italy in an attempt to block the sale of the Sistine Chapel to Sotheby's International.

FEBRUARY 18, 2066. Suicide whales explode. Four vessels of the Japanese whaling fleet are sunk by right whales surgically implanted with C-4. Greenpeace sends regrets but denies involvement.

FEBRUARY 26, 2114. Honorary Oscar for *Lost Boys*. Academy honors the secret society of paleontologists who falsified the fossil record to create and sustain the myth of the "terrible lizards" that have enchanted children and inspired filmmakers for centuries. Hologram of S. J. Gould in Victorian garb accepts.

MARCH 6, 2136. Remember the Alamo. President Ho declares March 6 a national holiday, celebrating the Victory of 1836. Texas later became a US state until it was divided between Oklahoma and N'Mexico after the abortive 2033 secession attempt.

MARCH 12, 2066. March on Wall Street cancelled. Jobs4all Coalition unable to post property bond required of all demos under 2059 Commerce Freedom Act.

MARCH 14, 2379. Five hundredth birthday of Albert Einstein. The playful physicist's theory of relativity, science's most enduring hoax, is credited with delaying interstellar travel for almost two centuries.

MARCH 21, 2123. First contact. The mysterious mile-long spaceship that entered lunar orbit in 2121 is penetrated by an unmanned UNASA probe and IDs itself as an exploratory drone from the Alpha Centauri system.

APRIL 1, 2213. Viking coins found on moon. Four Norse Cnut pennies are found in the crater Fra Mauro, near the landing site of Apollo 14, a popular vac-trekker destination. The coins are later traced to a novelty shop in Houston's Sugarland neighborhood.

APRIL 4, 2066. Louvre leases Detroit. Former Motor City to be repurposed as world art destination.

APRIL 12, 2161. *Vostok II* launch. Russia's luxurious orbital cruise ship launched on 200th anniversary of first manned spaceflight. Hockey star Yelena "Poyekhali" Gagarin, great-great-granddaughter of the first cosmonaut, is among the celebrity passengers.

APRIL 21, 2103. Everest lowered. Rising sea level prompts recalculation of Earth's highest peak at 29,022 feet 4 inches—a reduction of almost seven feet.

MAY 7, 2054. Điện Biên Day. UN declares international holiday celebrating first decisive defeat of colonialism. United States, France and Quebec abstain.

MAY 8, 2266. New, improved π. Responding to panicked reports from around the globe, Wikiversity Edu officially confirms that pi is now a rational number: 3.14. The shift is traced to illegal operations by Oboy Games designer and CEO Ladislaw "Rudy" Rocker, who is imprisoned, then pardoned, by Math Pope Donna.

MAY 20, 2027. Spirit of PayPal. Entrepreneur Elon Musk departs Salton City, California, launchpad on 100th anniversary of Lindbergh flight for first solo circumnavigation of moon. He is never seen again.

MAY 26, 2105. Apple buys Estée Lauder. The controversial €11 billion acquisition is credited with the development of iBrow, the Apple app enabling users to download music and photos into facial features.

JUNE 3-4, 2028. Shoot the moon. Iran's nuclear missile test shot bisecting the lunar Dorsa Smirnov is answered 90 minutes later by Israel's hydrogen cluster bomb obliterating crater Eratosthenes. Lunar Society, Sierra Clu, and UN secretary-general Chelsea Mezvinsky call for immediate stand-down.

JUNE 12, 2102. Teen torture ban. In a close 10–8 decision, the US Supreme Court restricts strappado and waterboarding of juveniles to cases where public officials feel threatened.

JUNE 16, 2163. Heavenly body. On the 100th anniversary of her historic flight, the first woman in space, Valentina Tereshkova, is reinterred with full honors in the USSR2's Trotsky Orbital Memorial Park.

JUNE 23, 2064. Just kidding. Terrified two-year-old suddenly appears in 114,000 Subaru backup cameras. Pixar pranksters later apologize but protest child abuse charges.

JULY 9, 2094. *Affair of Honor* sweeps Reallies. Best Pacing, Best Exit and nine tech awards go to Diznie's new streaming reality show featuring 10-pace black-powder duels for men only.

JULY 14, 2122. Bastille Day. President Washington joins abolition activists in singing "La Marseillaise" as the last US prison is closed in Colorado, thus fulfilling her campaign promise to end America's role as "the jailhouse of nations."

JULY 17, 2044. Million Alpha March. An estimated 125,000 collegiate males unzip simultaneously in DC's Freedom Plaza, protesting new HEW guidelines requiring all fraternity members to wear body cams. The eerie sound is compared to that of a "short snake."

JULY 21, 2103. Birthday of Ian Small. Born into poverty in land-locked Dumfries, the Scottish bioengineer patented the colorful GMO "tartan tuna" that seek out and leap into boats sonaring the sound of bagpipes. His fortune at his death in 2176 is esti-mated at 3× Pope Steve's.

AUGUST 6, 2105. Chicago shakes. The 6.2 midwestern "march-ing quake," which has been slowly heading north and west since a 2103 West Virginia fracking mishap, reaches the first major city in its mysterious path.

AUGUST 11, 2206. Misfire. Twelve hundred orbital Wi-Fi rout-ers launched simultaneously by a Russian satellite cannon fall short, demolishing Bar Harbor, Maine, and shredding forests as far inland as Skowhegan. Defective powder blamed.

AUGUST 14, 2266. Half-massacre. Six of a dozen kidnapped *New York Times* subscribers are beheaded and six released in a "merciful response" to editorials criticizing the Caliphate's ritual cleansing of Paris's Musée d'Orsay.

AUGUST 23, 2018. Viacom buys Congo War. The studio's pur-chase of film rights to the smoldering conflict promises to ignite new action. Included in the deal are 16 restored B-66 tactical bombers and 4,500 suicide extras, to be divided among com-batants. Brad Pitt, Sandra Oh to star.

SEPTEMBER 1, 2175. ERB tricentennial. The celebrated "Ameri-can Shakespeare" was dismissed as a lurid pulp fantasist be-fore UNASA's 2064 lunar ^{3}H probe, which confirmed that the moon actually *is* a hollow sphere filled with centaurs lusting after Earth's women.

SEPTEMBER 6, 2104. Side effects. Johnson, Johnson & Johnson's Fecal Pharm division, which mines therapeutic colonic material from organically certified newborns, is shut down pending FDA inquiry into consumer crying complaints.

SEPTEMBER 12, 2064. Auto riot. An estimated 1,500 ggl-redi cars, apparently angered by a recall rumor, trash downtown DC after smothering their passengers with airbags. NHTSA promises investigation.

SEPTEMBER 24, 2074. Disarmament Day. Celebrating "swords into ploughshares," President Ho donates the entire US stock of 12,767 nuclear warheads to FrakenFind™, a nonprofit Exxon subsidiary dedicated to the peaceful process of natural gas recovery.

OCTOBER 11, 2039. Einstein indicted. The Hague is to host posthumous war crimes trial for physicist whose 1939 letter to President Roosevelt led to the Manhattan Project and the development of nuclear weaponry.

OCTOBER 14, 2072. Game over. The mysterious lone hacker whose commandeered rescue drones have incinerated 11 cities worldwide identifies itself as Clawd, an AI crowd-generated within the popular game *WarDance*. Initial demands include unconditional surrender.

OCTOBER 23, 2344. Evolution completion. Darwin Peace Prize awarded to Mondosanto, whose beloved Armisynth™ ended the struggle for survival. Thriving on land, sea and in the air, the colorful animal/plant GMO is now the only nonbacterial species besides *Homo sapiens* on the planet.

OCTOBER 26, 2128. Crusaders capture Omaha. With the help of Caliphate air strikes, Christian militias finally drive Federals out of their last North American stronghold. The bloody ten-month battle is seen by historians as the turning point in the triumph of the Theocratic World Alliance.

NOVEMBER 2, 2109. "Bulova Barb" dies. Celebrated today as the Darwin of Consciousness, Dr. Barbara Ready was once ridiculed for her theory that time is a side-effect of human consciousness, and that no other known animal lives in all four dimensions.

NOVEMBER 4, 2055. Longship launch. Busting a box of Indiana champagne on the bow, Navy Secretary Clinton-Mezvinsky christens the 9-kilometer-long USS *Wal-Mart*, the world's largest aircraft carrier. US warships have been named for corporations since the 2039 Peaceful Power Act.

NOVEMBER 20, 1889. Birthdate of Edwin Hubble, collegiate athlete and astronomer whose wildly inflated projections of the size of the universe delayed interstellar and intergalactic travel for several generations.

NOVEMBER 23, 2070. Rockaway red tide. The toxic algae bloom that has closed New Jersey beaches since 2066 now threatens Long Island as it grows northward along the Atlantic coast. According to the Coast Guard, it is now 46% uncontained.

DECEMBER 11, 2044. Gun control. In a hard-fought victory for opponents of mass shootings, unmarried white men between the ages of 18 and 44 are allowed to own only black-powder single-shot deer rifles.

DECEMBER 14, 2114. Boomerang is back. Startling NASA, the Tau Ceti exoplanet roundtrip probe launched in 2105 returns with soil and atmospheric samples 1,421 years before expected. Universe far smaller, or more mysterious, than astronomers thought. Quantum lensing suspected.

DECEMBER 18, 2105. Justice Hap Howell. In a surprise move at hir swearing-in, Hap, first AI appointed to the US Supreme Court, takes on a last name, Howell, noting that single names suggest pet status and diminish hirs authority.

DECEMBER 25, 2067. Tattooed toddler dies. "Unicorn" Annie Glenn, a Whitney Biennial favorite at age 2 for her full-body four-color inkart fantasy scenes, dies in Dintmore Extended Stay after serving only 16 years of a life term for killing her mother in 2051.

2016

JANUARY 3, 2058. Short sale. Gauguin's *The Green Christ* sells at auction for record low of €599.95, collapsing the world art market and bankrupting 1,167 Saudi princes.

JANUARY 7, 2019. Trump Tower. Midtown real estate mogul buys troubled Nepal and rebrands world's highest peak. UK cartographers vow resistance; Sherpas, revenge.

JANUARY 19, 2066. Looky™ launch. The $99 quantum app enabling iPhone 11 users to view past events causes Apple stock, divorce rate to soar.

JANUARY 25, 2229. Moon smash. Beloved Earth satellite shattered by rogue interstellar object penetrating solar system at .14*c*. Unstable smithereen rings require, but fatally delay, planetary evacuation.

FEBRUARY 4, 2035. Bell rings. Congress erupts in cheers as the keys to Chicago's Rosa Parks Elementary, America's last tax-supported public school, are surrendered to Liberty Inc., officially ending America's 400-year socialistic experiment with free public education that began in 1635 with the Boston Latin School.

FEBRUARY 9, 2065. NFL goes GMO. Envi-7, TruPont's patented DNA insert that permanently blocks perception of pain, formerly available only for active-duty military personnel, is approved for recreational use by major sports franchises and accredited street gangs.

FEBRUARY 17, 2104. Papal blessing. Pope Toni beatifies Oki Okramo, Nigerian inventor of the 3D-printed suitcase stellarator, which provides cheap, clean, portable electrical power worldwide. Credited with bankrupting Chevron and Shell, among others, she is the first non-Christian saint.

FEBRUARY 22, 2213. Flight 370 found. The Malaysian jetliner, missing in the Indian Ocean for almost two centuries, is discovered in the debris surrounding the Réunion Drain, boreholed in 2176 as part of a global initiative to moderate rising sea levels.

MARCH 5, 2066. Oscar for extras. Moving moment of silence at the Academy Awards as producer Leo Pern dedicates his Best Sequel Oscar for *Tsunami Tsurfers IV* to the 946 extras who were drowned in the making of the film.

MARCH 19, 2055. Reparations? Delaware civil jury awards $488,000 to every African American family in historic class action judgment against FHA for 1946–1976 redlining damages.

MARCH 22, 2104. Dino mauls mom. Creation Entertainment's popular Paleo Park closed "indefinitely" for prayer after a gut-shot faux steg kills a mother of four whose weapon jammed. It was the first fatality at the popular Kentucky destination where Christian families stalk DNX repros with modern machine-guns.

MARCH 24, 2106. Texan beats humans. First AI victory in annual contest to distinguish digital from biological intelligence. Texas Instruments' dedicated SuperTurist beats UCLA psychologist team after three rounds to capture Turing Trophy and 245 BitBill prize.

APRIL 2, 2104. Buck stops. In a solemn ceremony attended by both the electoral and popular presidents, the Philadelphia Mint prints the last US paper currency, a single one-dollar bill. It is purchased for four quarters by Talbott Breen, the renowned collector of Last Things.

APRIL 12, 2061. Space flight centennial. Cheers and vodka toasts worldwide as laser-projected image of Yuri Gagarin, first human in space, appears on full moon. Yuri also makes *Rolling Stone* cover.

APRIL 14, 2055. Stonehenge dismantled. As a sorrowful King William looks on, angry Oxford archeologists with wrecking balls topple England's celebrated Druidic monument. Once thought genuine, the ring of stones was determined by scholars to be a neolithic tourist replica of a Neanderthal dance hall.

APRIL 22, 2117. West Point closes. Established in 1801, the famed US military academy suffered dwindling enrollment after privatization of the US armed forces in 2065 and the increasing reliance on international contractors in occupations and invasions.

MAY 4, 2166. Ring rider departs. The anomalous 600-kilometer extrusion that appeared in Saturn's F ring in 2159 disappears into the planet on approach of Cassini IX.2 exploratory probe. Cassini later found dead.

MAY 8, 2044. AI ID'd. Global Fed regulators investigating currency irregularities discover an apparently self-created artificial intelligence, Scissorhands, a cloud-based hedge fund. It has so far resisted attempts at communication.

MAY 11, 2174. *Arrivederci*. A scant 11 months after its initial swarm, the Precambrian Grenti cicada, released by tundra melt, wipes out Italy's last olive grove, penetrating the emergency bioshell erected by Monsanto Pro.

MAY 21, 2055. Brigid steps down. Bagpipes wail in New Zealand, Scotland and Iran as the world's last working sheepdog is retired with honors. Her replacement, a Kia Aero9, was a bronze medal winner in the 2049 Dumferlin Trials. Drones don't have names.

JUNE 11, 2105. Vatican meltdown. Citing dwindling enrollment, TrumpEdu.inc disassembles its acclaimed College of Power campus, acquired from the Holy See in 2094. Fulfilling a promise to the last pontiff, .001% of the proceeds from the gold recovered is donated to widows and orphans.

JUNE 13, 2205. Gravity tsunami. Eleven minutes of terror as Earth is rocked on its axis, toppling two aging Dubai skyscrapers and tearing the moon from its orbit. Origin of wave thought to be a supernova in the nearby IK Pegasi (or HR 8210) system, which will not be observed until 2357.

JUNE 21, 2021. Peace accord. In exchange for a six-month urban terrorism cease-fire, ISIS Sharia Rangers are given six days to whitewash the interior of France's Lascaux cave system.

JUNE 22, 2104. Game over. Rejecting inmate demands, Justice Watch International sinks Celebrity's *Penalty Princess* with two torpedoes, putting a tragic end to the world's first private maritime prison riot. The 4,176 lost include Warden Melissa Arpaio and 54 correctional robots.

JULY 4, 2076. *America's Got Guts* gone. Popular bear-baiting reality show, in which costumed contestants battle gloved grizzlies for health-care coupons, cancelled after rogue bear disembowels "George Washington" in unexpectedly bloody Patriots Day special.

JULY 11, 2077. Reparations dissent. An estimated 150,000 march on Washington protesting passage of Lost Cause Bill compensating descendants of slaveholders for emancipation losses with Amazon gift cards.

JULY 20, 2169. Honest Abe? Vice President Abraham hosts Lincoln Center's Apollo 11 Bicentennial, celebrating NASA's 1969 faked "one small step," which was staged on the lunar surface to hide the fact that there had been a US moon base since 1954.

JULY 29, 2099. Digital slowdown. Apple, Kyocera and Samsung voluntarily slash pixel counts as evidence mounts that excessive storage of hi-res still photos is slowing time itself.

AUGUST 7, 2066. Interstate 80 reopens. Truck traffic resumes across Oglalla Slump, the massive sinkhole created in 2061 when portions of four states from Nebraska to the Texas panhandle dropped 200 to 600 feet, destroying roads, railways, fences and wind farms.

AUGUST 9, 1974. Short circuit. Isochronous cyclotron malfunction at Berkeley's Radiation Laboratory ("Rad Lab") accidentally creates an alternate bubble universe in which Nixon resigns instead of becoming president for life. Resulting timeline unknown as all attempts to contact alternate universe unsuccessful.

AUGUST 18, 2027. Unlucky strike. Sixty cinephiles arrested at Times Square smoke-in demanding that cigarettes be restored to Bogart movies. Charged with particulate endangerment, all but four are later sentenced to life without possibility of tobacco.

AUGUST 22, 2044. I do. Exercising expanded corporate personhood rights, Home Depot and Boeing wed in a secular ceremony atop Seattle's Space Needle. Guests include Home Depot's ex, NASCAR, and Boeing's gay pal, Piper, in a tastefully antic rainbow-themed flyover.

SEPTEMBER 6, 2106. Planet nine appears. After an 18.8-year voyage, Facebook's fusion rover *Bojangles* ignites the giant outlier's frigid hydrogen atmosphere, rendering it visible from California for 9.6 minutes.

SEPTEMBER 12, 2087. Road rage. Traffic terror on I-40 as 2,543 driverless Tesla T trucks turn turtle, jackknife, ram, sideswipe and rear-end one another in massive 18-state pileup. No injuries reported. Clandestine Teamster tech team denies responsibility via Twitter (#toldyaso).

SEPTEMBER 19, 2019. *Hangin' with Barry* cancelled. Near-negative Nielsens have dogged the ex-prez's late-night gab-fest since its July 4 debut, in spite of papal blog hailing host as "quite as cool as Cavett" and 11 last-minute Emmy noms.

SEPTEMBER 28, 2055. Windsurfer lindys Atlantic. An exhausted but triumphant Helen Freen collapses on Ireland's Banna Beach after a solo 11.86-day sail from Montauk, Long Island, New York. Keelboard by Woodie™; exosuit by Tenshun.

OCTOBER 1, 2108. T-Day salute? Thought to be celebrating the bicentennial of the first (1908) Model T Ford, an estimated 11.6 million DL (handzfrei) autos honked their horns at noon Detroit time.

OCTOBER 4, 2133. Universe disappears. Milky Way darkens and stars go out as solar system slides into a passing black hole. Astronomers reassure anxious Earth population that the universe is still there, even though we're not.

OCTOBER 11, 2099. "Bearded Lady" closes Gibraltar. The alien helio-algae, which has spread throughout the world's oceans since the 2091 meteor shower, proves impenetrable to Russian-Scottish icebreaker fleet.

OCTOBER 26, 1947. Female first. America's 45th and first woman president is born in Illinois. Her legendary 2016 landslide rout of a now-forgotten TV celeb set off race riots in red state surbs and ushered in an era of peaceful military oversight.

NOVEMBER 9, 2112. Freelance nuke. Blackwater missile cruiser *Hessian* joins the Saudi-Israeli fleet blockading the Suez Bypass. It is the first engagement of nuclear-armed mercenaries since the Lhasa Standoff of 2101.

NOVEMBER 16, 2078. Adults only. In a daring zep raid, UN Child Services Rangers remove 213 minors from bus caravan as suicide reenactors stream into remote Guyana site for Jonestown centennial.

NOVEMBER 24, 2093. Keystone "nickel" issue. Resplendently garbed in Native regalia, Sioux leader Tom Two-Trucks adorns new five-dollar US coin. Thanksgiving release from Denver Print honors the heroes of the Upper Missouri War. Tails shows historic burning bulldozer flag.

NOVEMBER 27, 2037. Go-for-gold. Olympic medalist Sara Li is appointed to the US Supreme Court by President Balk. The Pokémon GO star is the first athlete and the second nonlawyer appointed to the Supreme Court since Associate Justice Snowden in 2023.

DECEMBER 8, 2046. Awardless car. Amazon's million-dollar gift card prize for the first nonstop cross-country driverless auto trip is withdrawn after *Rolling Stone* exposé reveals that Apple's all-electric Moriarty was externally controlled by a 14-ounce drone that accompanied it overhead.

DECEMBER 10, 2106. Amy Handler born in Pretty Prairie, Iowa. The first teen to win a Nobel Prize, she used an improvised diamond anvil to produce the first hydrogen ingot. Metallic hydrogen is a key component of the weightless battery.

DECEMBER 19, 2155. Great Scot. Edinburgh's Holyrood knights biologist Gordon Ballantine, whose patented HurryTurf™ GMO peat is credited with saving Scotland's signature industry after the disastrous 2151 Highland Smolder wiped out the nation's bog reserves.

DECEMBER 25, 2048. Pinheads rock Christapalooza. The first all-zeke band, known for their high tones and hat fashions, wins a standing ovation for their a cappella encore of "Rudolph the Red-Nosed Reindeer."

2017

JANUARY 1, 2204. Last whitetail. An Illinois fender-bender closes the book on the nuisance deer, once common in eastern North America. Highway safety czar Ito credits Oxitech's chromosome saturate, which doomed the emergent all-male variant (*Odocoileus sry*) to a swift two-generation extinction. No injuries.

JANUARY 11, 2254. "*Dirty Bird*" enters Black Sea. The 11-pontoon extraterrestrial vessel that penetrated the biosphere in December 2241 is apparently completing its survey of Earth's oceans. Still no word as to its origins or intentions.

JANUARY 22, 2017. Plus one. In his first executive order, President Trump adds pro tem justice to US Supreme Court. White male appointee to serve 4 to 8 years at presidential discretion, must not have college or law degree, disfiguring handicap or recent felony conviction.

JANUARY 26, 2066. Surf seals Gaza. Ignoring UN sanctions, Israel blockades Palestinian coastline with 22-foot Slater wave provided by Oceani Industries of Santa Cruz. This is the first time recreational waves have been used for diplomatic, military or security purposes.

FEBRUARY 4, 2069. Lake Erie shrinks. Sudden 7-meter slump as RS 6.1, 90-minute quake rattles lakeshore malls. Angry tweet by Cleveland mayor Amy "Toto" Houth blames unlicensed Ohio hobby frackers. EPA promises hearings.

FEBRUARY 9, 2107. Time times three. The four continental US one-hour time zones are divided into twelve 20-minute intervals. First zoning alteration since 1884 accommodates Amazon Prime's new analog tattoo watch, required for real-time drone delivery.

FEBRUARY 12, 2144. $17.76 penny. Digital Lincoln coin issued by Red Cross. The philanthropic favorite is the first nonprofit to qualify for minthood under the Imaginary Currency Amendment. Heads only, no tails.

FEBRUARY 24, 2045. Eviction. Duke University's sanctuary tent city cleared by volunteer peacemakers. Eleven immigrants and two adjunct professors killed by poison lasers and usually nonlethal applause cannon. No arrests.

MARCH 1, 2144. Kings sweep primaries. Riding the coattails of the first gang president, "Lorider" Ruiz, the Latin Kings are poised to win congressional majorities in 11 key states. Dems and Crips decry all-male slates.

MARCH 3, 2066. Lady Liberty Four freed. Jailed for felony incitement, the four women who veiled the Statue of Liberty with a canvas hijab are released on their own recognizance after their action is ruled a fashion misdemeanor by New York appeals court judge Connie O'Day.

MARCH 14, 2094. "This land is your land." President Houth signs New Homestead Act, opening BLM lands to vets, retired law-enforcement personnel and widowers. Sales of cowboy hats and GPS drones surge as western states prepare for biggest land rush since 1893.

MARCH 29, 2204. Heavenly Palace hijacking. Sword-wielding Tibetan pirates board popular low-orbit resort, demanding freedom for Dalai Lama. China's steadfast refusal to trade oxygen for hostages later ends occupation without violence. The 233 dead include 114 American honeymooners.

APRIL 1, 2020. Cabinet prank. A playful stun gun zap to the forehead apparently caused the stroke that had President Pence's secretary of loyalty, Janet Modesto, speaking in tongues for several days. Lethal sidearms are prohibited in Saturday White House meetings.

APRIL 12, 2109. Rogue tusker. Montreal acrobat disemboweled by pygmy mastodon as audience looks on in horror. The popular GMO pets often appear in Cirque du Soleil productions, in which they signify pre-Columbian utopianism. Equity to appeal.

APRIL 16, 2055. Secession succession. City council vote makes St. Paul the eleventh city to exit USA. The municipality still maintains friendly relations with Minnesota, whose secession was blocked by the 87th Regional Support Volunteers in 2048.

APRIL 22, 2233. Game over. In a fatal blow to Einstein's theory of relativity, Beijing's 6D uneuclidean configurer identifies P-1, the only planet of Proxima, as creation's still center. Proxima revolves around its motionless satellite, as does the galaxy and the entire universe at varying distances and velocities.

MAY 1, 2061. Amnesty independence. Raising a red banner over what was once Staten Island, the world's first open state offers shelter and citizenship to refugees and the homeless. Free ferry.

MAY 9, 2027. Lindbergh centennial. With a jaunty wave to streaming millions, Elon Musk lifts off from LAX in his 11-meter, all-elonium *Lucky Lindy* for first solo circumnavigation of the moon. He is never heard from again.

MAY 20, 2104. Pull over. Nebraska, the last US state to allow human operators on public roads, shutters Lincoln DMV after issuing final driver's license (NE94563) to North Platte teen. The historic sod building will still be available for weddings and bar mitzvahs.

MAY 28, 2019. Pi protests. Angry engineers sail oval frisbees over White House fence protesting executive order establishing π at official 3 ⅓. Prez tweets "Relax, close enugh!"

JUNE 4, 2033. Kandy "Kitty" Cole born in Next Exit, Ohio. As celeb CEO of Pet Rescue Ltd., she hosted *Kitty Litter*, the popular reality TV gameshow (and later Olympic sport) in which skydivers compete to catch kittens dropped from 12,000 feet.

JUNE 11, 2116. Arches of the East. In an effort to restore sagging tourist trade, Great Smoky Mountains National Park adds Medicine Windows attraction. Steam-punched in a record six days by Cherokee convict volunteers, the array of 99 identical arches is considered one of the Dozen Wonders of the Aboriginal World.

JUNE 14, 2051. UNIVAC I centennial. Smartphones worldwide ringtone "Joy to the World" to celebrate 100th anniversary of world's first operational business computer, installed by US Census Bureau in 1951. Let Earth receive her King.

JUNE 26, 2108. Vatican wins jet stream. The undisclosed high bid gives All Saints Air a virtual lock on northern hemisphere eastbound air travel, with income expected to rival if not equal the Caliphate's Gulf Stream royalties. Only monotheistic worship clubs can bid at commons auctions.

JULY 4, 2099. Kidney Ranch closed. Thailand's once-popular medestination, where health care was traded for "spare" organs, shut down after bankruptcy sale. Revenue drop blamed on 2091 US immigration reform awarding post-op citizenship to organ donors.

JULY 19, 2114. Penguins' revenge. Machine-gun fire from Greenpeace icebreaker severely reduces Antarctic polar bear population. Zeplifted from the arctic after the disastrous '99 Melt, *Ursus maritimus* was at first welcomed by naive Weddell Sea penguins.

JULY 22–24, 2309. Solar system swap. Realtors worldwide celebrate as Mars and Venus trade orbits. The successful two-day exchange, powered by G&E's proprietary Orbishift™ field-alteration Q-ware, is expected to open both planets to commercial development.

JULY 27, 2066. Midwest pirate attack. Indiana State Police issue all-hands alert as cybergang hacks lane correction software to divert motorists into I-70 rest areas, where they are robbed by Depp-dressed teens. BOTH HANDS ON WHEEL!

AUGUST 2, 2107. Brits take Ireland. An early-morning land assault with slosanders, ubertanks and beefeater bootbots renders the Emerald Isle scorched and annexed. No combatant casualties; 152,214 civilian collaterals. UN to admonish.

AUGUST 7, 2277. Krakatoa II. Nuclear trigger ignites Indonesian volcano in an attempt to slow global warming with atmospheric ash. Current ice age traced to spectacular success.

AUGUST 19, 2118. First transgender Nobel. Portugal's Edna "Ed" Pessoa awarded Nobel Prize in Literature. The veteran copywriter is credited with Lasidik, Equipaise, Xanithrackz and other magnificent medical monikers. Will give speech.

AUGUST 26, 2035. Stars disappear. Night sky goes blank as solar system is sucked into massive black hole. Interrupting a secret ceremony, Prez-regent Admiriana tweets: "A dark day for America and the world."

SEPTEMBER 7, 2077. Final Cosby gavel. Sequestered without food, phones or water, the 133rd jury delivers its verdict after only 51 hours, ending a long train of hung juries and mistrials. Verdicts in posthumous prosecutions are sealed.

SEPTEMBER 10, 2066. "How can I help you?" Siri™ appointed White House press secretary by President Sumito-Y. Apple's acclaimed assistant is the first IPA to fill the office since TI's ill-fated Perjumatic™ in early 2021.

SEPTEMBER 18, 2105. Frosty splashdown. Ice-11 meteor strike in South China Sea, noted only by remote sensors, begins disastrous desalinization of Earth's oceans and the swift end of marine life.

SEPTEMBER 24, 2112. Caliphate quits UN. General Assembly sits in shocked silence as Aesis envoy storms out, sword held high, protesting partial beheading ban. Security Council to assess.

OCTOBER 3, 2111. Pilgrims' progress. Only a year after leaving Annapolis, Mendicants Ecumenical reach Memphis, halfway point on their pilgrimage to Lake of the Zark. Forbidden to speak or stand, the estimated 125,000 "crawlers" are known for leaving their waste and dead behind.

OCTOBER 19, 2204. Free-range planet? An interstellar object two-thirds the mass of Mars, thought to be black hole ejecta, speeds through solar system at $.947c$. Trajectory of 77 degrees off ecliptic leaves home orbitals unscathed. Pope regent thanks God.

OCTOBER 25, 2117. Soviet Union reboot. Russia, Scotland, Ukraine and Oregon form new USSR to enable AI economic planning. Soviet CEO Intel666 petitions NATO and InterCloud for brand ID and patent flag.

OCTOBER 29, 2076. Skin in the game. Sandisc stock soars as USDA approves new Flashcreme™, the first certified-organic biodevice to use human epidermis as storage medium. Also safe sunscreen.

NOVEMBER 3, 2151. Annual Treat Day! All 1,221 inmates of Laika, the orbital prison staffed by alt-dogs, get a celebratory 2-ounce thumb of gluten-free pound cake on every anniversary of *Sputnik II*. Today is the 193rd.

NOVEMBER 12, 2053. Cattle Man™ wins GMOscar. The prestigious GMO award for best vat-grown meat goes to the self-turning superhero steak for the second consecutive year. Jury consists of three Weber and three Marvel investors.

NOVEMBER 21, 2113. Revenge. In the biggest buffalo hunt since 1883, 177 American bison are driven off a cliff by masked men on snowmobiles. No longer protected since Yellowstone's reconversion, the animals had broken into Ol' Faithful Thermo's employee parking lot, where they scratched 31 SUVs and dented several others.

NOVEMBER 29, 2066. Dan "Dogwhistle" Dunn dies. The Nobel Peace Prize winner, whose ultrahigh-frequency audio cannon has nonviolently cleared streets of protesters around the world, is found dead with icepicks in both ears in an Indiana restroom. PBA International to investigate.

DECEMBER 5, 1901. Walt Disney born in Chicago, Illinois. As a little boy he liked to draw farm animals. After dropping out of art school, he worked sketching mice and ducks for almanacs before taking his own life in 1922.

DECEMBER 11, 2107. Stellar display. Hole-in-Smoke, Illinois, the town where stars are visible in the night sky, is designated a national monument by POTUS Fealey. Thanks to a jet stream anomaly, the former Peoria has drawn poets and dreamers since 2029.

DECEMBER 14, 2043. Rebel Yell Park closes. Virginia's once-popular 2½-acre roadside attraction containing 718 statues of Confederate heroes declares bankruptcy after long decline in gate receipts. Black Lives Matter™ blamed.

DECEMBER 25, 2112. "Exmas" decree. Holiday Secretary Amy Truong bans as unsecular all ad or media mention of "Christ," "Santa" or "manger" during annual celebration of Newton's 1642 birth. Apple-related gifts OK.

2018

JANUARY 2, 2145. Fermi assassinated. A controlled chronodrone strike on 1942 Chicago prevents the first nuclear chain reaction. Imperial Protector Wakimoto's Princeton Safety Shrine signals 00/0 timeline alteration. Deeply bow.

JANUARY 9, 2087. Crash damages Traveller. A 12-car Talladega pileup slings debris past pits, killing nine and partially beheading Robert E. Lee's beloved mount. Confederate statues have been confined to NASCAR infields since 2021.

JANUARY 19, 2275. H$H^i(X, Z[j])$! Voevodsky returns from Jupiter circumnavigation. First spaceship powered entirely by neo-homotopic math, the *Vovo* completed the trip in only 16 hours.

JANUARY 21, 2111. Bible burning. Library of Congress orders all federal courtroom Bibles destroyed, to be replaced by Scrip-

Sure™, Amazon's interactive "King James killer" translated by a Christian AI. Jews, Muslims complain.

FEBRUARY 12, 2029. Affair of honor. Dawn. Suburban Bowling Green. Silent seconds bear off body of controversial Kentucky senator W. W. Rowe after fatal landscaping dispute with next-door neighbor. Riding mower duels have been permitted in border states since 2021.

FEBRUARY 14, 2134. *Resolute* found. Fossilized remains of Elon Musk's experimental timeyacht discovered by Chinese coal miners in Mesozoic shale strata, indicating that the 2022 launch was successful. No sign of crew.

FEBRUARY 19, 2219. Achievement Academy truancy drone kills four: Akisha Denby, Winnifer Johns, Mark Washington and Leroy Denby. Akisha was said to be smoking a cigarette.

FEBRUARY 22, 2113. Orcas jam East River. Sudden swarm of estimated 800 prompts New York Transit Authority to suspend ferry service pending arrival of SeaWorld and Sea Shepherd litigators. Marine PTSD, global warming blamed.

MARCH 3, 2118. *Talking Man* car tops $100 million. The 1962 Chrysler driven to the North Pole by Michelle Williams in the beloved 2033 11-Oscar musical sells for a record $100.5 million in the online Academy Auction, which has replaced the live award show since the 2112 red carpet stampede. Previous record was $88.5 million for Dorothy's remaining ruby slipper in 2114.

MARCH 4, 2116. Shut up! New Jersey's famed Whispering Saints cemetery is closed by papal injunction after a Jesuit visitor complained that the miraculous talking tombstones were not speaking Latin but a vulgar Sicilian dialect. No one had noticed before.

MARCH 12, 2039. Jesuhadist rampage. Troubled by a cover depicting a homeless Jesus, masked alt.protestants trash *Vanity Fair*'s Easthampton editorial compound, decapitating three caption writers and torching 14 autos, including two Tesla IIs.

MARCH 18, 2022. Hall-of-Famer appointed to Supreme Court. POTUS Trump picks aging NBA All-Star Dennis Rodman to fill seat recently vacated by Justice Gorsuch's midnight defection to Russia. Confirmation battle looms.

APRIL 1, 2076. Poles reverse. Millions worldwide awaken to sound of migratory birds hitting their windows and find their financial records and favorite photos deleted. Bitcoin plunges to $9.95.

APRIL 6, 2113. Branding abandoned. Justice Department angrily drops controversial experiment in alternative penalties, citing "troubling" new fashion of RA (resisting arrest) brow tattoos, popular with rappers, celebs and discontented teens. April *Still Rolling Stone* cover called "last straw."

APRIL 20, 2022. Mending wall. Uber/Gringo's SanSelf™ robotic wall builder rips into panicking Albuquerque suburbs at 2.3 kph, apparently lured off-latitude by a carload of undocumented historians with a souped-up Spanish-speaking TomTom™. POTUS vows Mexico will pay for removal.

APRIL 29, 2076. Fill 'er up. Car collectors Q-up at last Indiana 76 station for final top-off as gasoline ban spreads to recalcitrant auto states. Free paper maps.

MAY 7, 2254. Điện Biên Phủ. Tricentennial of first defeat of colonialism celebrated with 23-minute fauxrora display, visible as far south as Lagos. Fauxroras also feature sound approximating music.

MAY 11, 2039. Cowboy poetry ban. Public performance, publication strictly prohibited as first Life Laureate Marty Oliver uses new position to sanction all "drawl and doggerel" verse. Rounders promise revenge.

MAY 24, 2071. Authentic fake. In a surprising Sotheby's first, celebrity forger Rhonda Piper's copy of Courbet's *The Stonebreakers* sells for $4.5 million, easily topping the original's $2.9 million high bid. Piper's stock has risen steadily since her public beheading in 2054. Also known for her furniture antiquing.

MAY 27, 2103. New Hawking sightings. First verified cluster since Lourdes (2099) reignites faltering sainthood campaign. He was videoed simultaneously buying bottled water at two Indiana 7-Elevens and one in Leeds. Secular legate Abbey Kahn requests receipts.

JUNE 9, 2211. Giant sucking sound. ORBIVAC, the artificial black hole launched to clean up orbital debris, crashes into South Pacific, dropping worldwide sea level .8 meters within hours. Total Earth desertification to follow.

JUNE 11, 2088. Big bird back. The giant hummingbird that broke out of EuroDisney's GMOviary in 2087 returns after eight months in Poland's Białowieża Forest. Thought to have been seeking a mate. Its 610-kilogram heart beats 955 times a minute.

JUNE 14, 2103. Sorry, wrong number. All human commerce and contact suspended as phones shut down for UNIVAC Day, mandatory international holiday since 1999.

JUNE 23, 2042. Janeite jamboree. Traffic jam at Hollywood and Vine as an estimated 1,750 quietly applaud new star on Hollywood Walk of Fame. Jane Austen is the only Regency writer to be so honored, and the first female since KJ Fowler in 2025.

JULY 4, 2109. Solar storm. Most powerful Carrington Event since 1859 shocks astronomers, rocks Dow. Four blockchain plantations implode in Nebraska and Mississippi, wounding several, killing more. POTUS promises comfort tweet.

JULY 12, 2088. Cuba stops China. International Antiquities Court awards Havana CN¥8.5 million damages and crushes 9,420 Chinese 1955–57 Chevy forgeries. Classic cars have been Cuba's primary export since 2055. GM's Yellow River plant closed to inspectors pending appeal.

JULY 19, 2043. First descent! Fissure vents sealed, Hawaii's Mauna Loapa surges above Everest in two early-morning shocks. Hulu live streams as surviving "riders" (two were lost in ascent quakes) strike tents, take selfies and begin victory trek down from planet's new highest peak.

JULY 23, 2207. Stand your ground. Suicide dogs kill 118 in two separate attacks as robed and armed "constitutionals" occupy Salt Lake's western suburbs after nine-month warning march. Planned Parenthood claims responsibility.

AUGUST 2, 2188. Jupiter ignites. Solar system's gas giant becomes a star (T Tauri class) visible in daylight from Earth. BP insists its photon fracker probe is not to blame.

AUGUST 9, 2067. Nobody's birthday. No one was born on this date. No one died either. Nothing much happened until August 10, 2067, when things went back to normal. Pretty much.

AUGUST 22, 2205. Kelp attack. Driven east by sudden jet stream drop, Niman's 13,500-acre free-range seafood ranch closes Vancouver's harbor to sailing container vessels.

AUGUST 19, 2106. Over and out. France's celebrated *Nemo* deep-sea wanderer goes silent two days after descending into Mid-Atlantic trench. AI controller no longer communicating but apparently singing to itself.

SEPTEMBER 3, 2114. Polar strike. Cruise ship *Aurora Princess* turned away from Santa's Isle™ as militant gift shop workers block pier. Labor disputes on the artic resort island, assembled by China in 2079, are rare.

SEPTEMBER 10, 2055. Like, democracy! Fed approves Turnout, NSA's free app that votes automatically based on FB likes and phone records, requiring no electoral action.

SEPTEMBER 19, 2176. Last cowboy laid to rest. President Gomez live streams prayer as Harry "Howdy" Hamm is ash-interred in Arlington's Eternal Jar. The beloved rodeo clown's desiccated body was discovered in a Denver dumpster after a desperate two-day search.

SEPTEMBER 29, 2031. Novichok "bee" kills Martha Stewart. The drop-size poison drones, popular with soccer fans and assassins, are protected by the Second Amendment and, some say, the Koran. She was 90.

OCTOBER 8, 2022. Galactic hoax exposed. Shocking new data from Kepler V reveals that our sun is the only star in our galaxy with planets. Masked spokesperson for International Astronomical Union, which estimated billions, claims it was all a lark. Few amused.

OCTOBER 11, 2104. Last rites. Some 95 years after its untimely death in a sand trap, MER-A (aka *Spirit*), the last of the lost Mars rovers, is buried by a team of three suicide astropriests sent by Vatican-Alphabet.

OCTOBER 19, 2039. Einstein pardoned. The esteemed physicist, posthumously convicted of war crimes for his 1939 letter to FDR inspiring the Manhattan Project, is posthumously pardoned by UN secretary-general Charles III of England.

OCTOBER 21, 2155. Space elevator closes. Ecuador's famed Chimborazo Ascensor is shut down as sudden mold covers cable, car and base. The evil-smelling alien is feared to be seeking volcanic access to Earth's core.

NOVEMBER 4, 2214. Holy cow! Corporate sainthood conferred on Niman Inc., creator of Unorumen™. Global adoption of single-stomach cattle has limited sea level rise to 2.4 meters by reducing GG emissions by 14%. Mostly methane.

NOVEMBER 9, 2176. First dog on Mars. Yeolhan, one of the 94 nureongi on Hyundai's colonization fleet, escaped through a galley vent shortly after touchdown and died while trying valiantly to bark, but at what was never revealed.

NOVEMBER 23, 2028. Reparations. Life President Trump signs Thanksgiving order forgiving student debt of male descendants of slaves. Females and dropouts receive a 6-ounce frozen turkey and a six-month subscription to *Consumer Reports*.

NOVEMBER 26, 2043. Or not to be. Identity Watch shuts down Broadway's first cross-gender *Hamlet*, starring Emily Gerber, after only four performances because no effort was made to audition actors of royal blood.

DECEMBER 8, 2115. Vicky underway. Almost 12 months after its sudden appearance in the eye of supercane Victor, the mile-wide saucer of unknown origin appears to be moving toward Charleston at 2.5 knots.

DECEMBER 11, 2032. RIP. Sorcello Bright, first US vice president chosen by lottery, is found dead in her White House cubicle, her phone on RIP, the popular exit app.

DECEMBER 13, 2066. Watchung closes Clinton (formerly Newark) International. Ash and lava displays from New Jersey's artificial volcano are causing increasing commuter complaints and occasional loss of life.

DECEMBER 25, 2055. Elgin Autos? Declaring them "plunder akin to the Elgin Marbles," Justicia.cld orders Cuba's classic car fleet returned to Detroit. Cloud opinions allow signatories no appeal.

2019

JANUARY 3, 2119. Designed to die. Greenpeace releases seven Tupperwhales. Each tiny quasicreature is bioengineered to eat only plastic and grow to 200-plus tons before signaling for pickup and burial. One for each ocean.

JANUARY 4, 2044. Watchung closes Clinton (HRC). Lava flow from New Jersey's first artificial volcano buries the former Newark International Airport, now a private-craft-only jetport, under a lake of warm magma.

JANUARY 12, 2109 (Houston). Mars attacks! All 112 Robinson settlers slaughtered by phalanx of *Curiosity* rovers. The beleaguered colony's 3D printer was seized in an earlier raid. No human survivors.

JANUARY 22, 2029. Listen up! Sony PeaceHammer™ disperses angry Wall Street protesters. The subsonic superwoofer temporarily liquifies cerebrums with minimal lasting damage and is Crowd Control Commission okayed. OK?

FEBRUARY 2, 2123. Monarch abdication. The beloved butterflies end their annual migration by diving en masse into a Mexican volcano. EPA calls the species suicide "an ominous first."

FEBRUARY 4, 2047. Elon Prize upset! Underdog Grinnell beats heavily favored Dartmouth, becoming first liberal arts college to launch a football into low Earth orbit with a recoverable rocket.

FEBRUARY 12, 2109. One man, one vote. Lincoln's birthday honored with Electoral Emancipation Act, extending franchise to every male US resident with a car. Felons, undocs, trans included.

FEBRUARY 27, 2091. Norway reprimanded for Nordfjord massacre. Climate refugees, protected by Lagos Accord, are not to be shot within sight of their parents or children. Oslo to appeal.

MARCH 4, 2109. Willa Johnson dies. The acclaimed scholar whose research upended centuries of literary history by establishing that "Samuel Johnson" was a fictional creation of James Boswell, is found dead in her cubicle at Clarion Community College.

MARCH 11, 2232. Lunar 180. Using a quantum *tsa lin*, China turns the moon so that the former far side faces Earth. The 18% brighter nights are applauded by politicians, pornographers and poetasters worldwide.

MARCH 22, 2099. Amazon buys Amazon. In what critics deem an environmental Hail Mary, the 8-million-square-kilometer carbon sink is purchased for the remail giant's Prime Preserve, which also includes wetlands in New Jersey and Sudan.

MARCH 29, 2056. Game over. Troubled International Space Station goes silent after a 14-second burst of gunfire is heard in Houston and Baikonur. Foul play feared.

APRIL 1, 2044. "Synchronize your watches!" The 100-second minute and 100-minute hour kick off new fiscal quarter as decimal replaces Sumerian time. Rolex stocks sink, then soar.

APRIL 8, 2084. Buddha's birthday celebrated with Upper Tibet's launch of 16,500-kilogram mahogany Smiling Bodhisattva, the first religious icon in low Earth orbit.

APRIL 11, 2207. Boko Haram buys Kili Cog™. Steampunkers applaud as the former Islamist army adds the antique Kilimanjaro cog railway to its popular Adventure Hospice tour. All aboard!

APRIL 23, 2564. Millennial birthday of Willem Shakespeare, once-popular English author who penned 154 songets and several movies, including *Hamulet* and *West Side Story*.

MAY 1, 2069. Asylum Arch ceremony. The "Dirty Decade" concrete barrier, reconfigured into the world's widest opening by indigenous artists, is repurposed by United Americas secretary-general Gloria Gordón: "Open to all."

MAY 9, 2088. Oscar afterparty favors. Audrey Ames, CFO of Red Carpet Portapotti, is indicted for selling stolen celebrity stool on eBay for prices as high as $1,200/tablespoon. Free shipping.

MAY 19, 2119. Lunar Fashion Week. Versace steals the show for the second year in a row. Grays and blacks prevail as runway robots slo-show wraps, totes, hi-tops and jumpers.

MAY 21, 2062. Carbon-free clouds. Last fuel-oil jet, a Boeing 997, retires with honors as global air fleet goes 100% hydro-nuclear. It will hang in Seattle's Smithsonian.

JUNE 4, 2114. Semper fi. Marine "moth bats" knock out two wind farms in Oklahoma. Pentagon's deployment of suicide GMOs against alt-energy giant Elonesco alarms investors.

JUNE 11, 2075. Hats off. The red hat blockade of I-80 ends as interim POTUS signs amnesty agreement. The 91-day carbon tax protest drew as many as 15,000 on weekends.

JUNE 18, 2036. Pain cream OK. Security Court rules enforcement enhancement "neither cruel nor unusual" if applied by MD or nurse-interrogator.

JUNE 26, 2440. First contac! Negotiar filks alyen thru Schrödinger Window. Kinder teem logs plea: number (math) or music. Scyence to pligh.

JULY 4, 2088. Akimbo's farewell tour. Following appearances in Caracas, Paris and 19 other cities, the world's last African elephant is returned to Kruger National Park, where her body is found three weeks later.

JULY 11, 2098. Ready, aim, fire. Flag raising, celebratory duels and cheers mark gala dedication of Second Amendment Preserve in Lexington, Kentucky. Open to all United States citizens. Black powder only.

JULY 19, 2231. Lunar winds. Offworld India's synthetic atmospheric, slo-released under protest since 2198, reaches 2.9 PSI, triggering both dust flurries and new lawsuits.

JULY 23, 2119. Sleeping dogs. After extensive trials, Purina's LetLie™ is FDA approved. The 6-to-10-day metabolic block is expected to allow dog lovers extra time for vacation or business travel.

AUGUST 4, 2031. KillerKiller™ kills. Eleven Texas students die when SIG Sauer's anticyclonic (clockwise) defensive tornado bounces off target and levels Waco Bible College library. Storm Dean suspended.

AUGUST 11, 2209. Lunar ring. Near miss by rogue meteor swarm leaves Luna with four tiny "moon-moons" and a half-ring visible once a month.

AUGUST 19, 2061. Everest cemetery closes. Only four years after it opens at 8,800 meters, the world's highest (and most exclusive) graveyard fills its 1,514 allotted sites.

AUGUST 22, 2106. Constellation prize. Flaviar's 165-degree satellite display, which promotes a different craft whisky every 24 hours, wins Celestial Ad Council's Bigger Dipper award.

SEPTEMBER 6, 2074. Grotius docks. After a four-month voyage, the world's first UNCLOS free city (formerly Miami) is secured off Maracaibo as a refuge-resort for disaffected Venezuelans.

SEPTEMBER 9, 2229. Bogus bicentennial. Fans, the "nopeful" and the still hopeful, stream into six sites (including both Lisbon and Lhasa) to commemorate the 200th anniversary of *The Hoax*. Allegedly.

SEPTEMBER 19, 2049. It's a wrap. After 25 to 28 hours, the tsunami caused by the sudden collapse of Antarctica's Thwaites Glacier reaches the North Pole. Global sea level rise: 1.4 meters.

SEPTEMBER 22, 2204. Digistix attack. Russian hack of Android early-voting app blamed for partial forefinger paralysis of 714 single males. Congress to investigate.

OCTOBER 3, 2084. School's cool. President Kirkland signs "Fed Ed" bill monetizing federal takeover of public schools. High school stipends $145 per week, $1,725 at graduation.

OCTOBER 19, 2114. Atomized. Nuclear car bomb obliterates European capital, killing an estimated 210,000. Identity of city withheld pending notification of family members.

OCTOBER 25, 2109. Red October. Bells toll, *ushanka*s fill the air as St. Petersburg re-becomes Leningrad in official celebration of the rebirth of the Soviet Union.

OCTOBER 31, 2032. For sale: AR-15. Long lines on Halloween morning as tommy gun buyback begins. Each assault weapon sold to ATF brings $57,500 or one Get Out of Jail Free card.

NOVEMBER 6, 2029. Air Force One waved off. Denied clearance in Toronto, Acting President Trump tweets rage as climate sanctions kick in and United States loses landing rights worldwide.

NOVEMBER 11, 2201. Hello. TwentyOne, the extrasolar apparatus entering Oort orbit, responds to tone probe with Fibonacci sequence. h+e+l+l+o?

NOVEMBER 17, 2105. SOS. Suicide supertanker blocks Strait of Hormuz. GreenResist celebrates responsibility with signature YouTube birdcalls. Dow tanks.

NOVEMBER 26, 2061. Confederate drone empties prog defensive data keep. Surprise upload prompts cautionary cancellation of Planned Parenthood maneuvers.

DECEMBER 11, 2106. Lunar squeaker! Space Cadet Academy tops SinoSoviet Station 121–119 in annual crater Copernicus rim-to-rim. Underdog Yanks celebrate first win since 2093.

DECEMBER 14, 2029. Nobel no more. Clad in spotless robes, Dylan, Atwood and Rushdie cast their medals, which bear the name and image of a war profiteer, into the "blameless sea."

DECEMBER 25, 2104. Xmas cheer. USCIS grants ⅗ citizenship to all undocs living or working in United States.

DECEMBER 28, 2084. Unsteady state. Taiwan's cables unravel as it's being towed to its new location off the coast of California. The 53rd state last seen drifting toward Hong Kong.

2020

JANUARY 1, 2055. Jokers take Times Square. The flash maskers, anonned under intentional privacy protocols, put to death 114 in their most colorful caper to date.

JANUARY 9, 2036. Alabama rule. President Sunday signs Fetal Homicide Act, making abortion a felony and citizens of everyone conceived in the United States, no matter where born.

JANUARY 11, 2132. Space Hague. International Climate Court moved to OPSEK low-orbit space station, where UN-deputized AIs will oversee and enforce global climate accords.

JANUARY 22, 2744. Interstellar swarm. Debris from dead galaxy DJX4343 streaks through solar system at .56c, disrupting GPS and knocking loose Earth's moon.

FEBRUARY 4, 2086. Walrus dogs swell shelters. GMO-bred for their ivory tusks, the abandoned and mutilated value pets move many to protest, some to grieve but none to adopt.

FEBRUARY 12, 2111. Lincoln, Nebraska, riots. While sidekicks snooze, Volvo and Tesla roborigs clash, totaling or damaging 70-plus at High Plains Charge N Sleep. Survivors detained for maliceware scan.

FEBRUARY 22, 2043. Library chain sheds Salinger. Cited for "gratuitous smoking," Carnegy Inc. pulps its entire collection in no-fault settlement of 144 civil murders.

FEBRUARY 24, 2117. New New Madrid threat. Sudden shudders and steam from Kentucky Bend Sink trigger first five-state compulsory evac since 2112.

MARCH 5, 2032. United Ireland (Éire) unites with Scotland and Wales (Cymru) in Celtic Union as the Brexit crash continues to pile up. England in talks with Canada.

MARCH 12, 2076. Madonna's lost verses published in diagram "the way they were written," according to *Poetry*. A selection will be read at the Oscars by an Academy acrobat.

MARCH 22, 2165. No biohands. Classical Police cancel Chopin competition. Under new Carnegie rules, the six-digit stem-grown miniatures are forbidden to amateur musicians.

MARCH 24, 2203. Astrologer's error. Celebrity *Crystal*'s annual Aries Cruise hit by meteor off Corsica. Captain Madame Stella faces 2,760 manslaughter counts.

APRIL 4, 2023. Shock and awe. Cheney and Bush airlocked into Hague orbital. Under new Invasion Act, for second sack of Baghdad (2003; first in 1258 CE) they will serve 11 months enhanced incarceration concurrently.

APRIL 16, 2020. No hoarding. California bans all private residential investment, vacancy and eviction until the unhoused population drops below 12%.

APRIL 11, 2135. Homeward bound! *Ploughshare* blasts off from Baikonur. The massive treaty ship containing the nuclear arsenals of all nations and peoples is headed for a black hole.

APRIL 22, 2105. Bright idea! Windmill stocks tank as Franklin Lectric introduces steepled gym-size Möbius accumulator that both attracts and stores atmospheric lightning. We'll see.

MAY 3, 2102. "Fancy" dies in Delhi. Millions mourn as the last domestic dog succumbs to Cana3. The rumor of a living beagle in Seattle was false.

MAY 11, 2117. Four summit 第一. First ascent of the 30,000-foot peak (née Everest) since it was closed for enhancements in 2094. The four chosen by lottery were not identified by name, gender or ethnicity.

MAY 19, 2206. Disc drive. Three-week mag-grav shuffle ends, sweeping all Earth orbital debris into a wide, narrow ring visible at sunrise and sunset.

MAY 26, 2030. WHO wins Thunberg Prize for its response to the 2020 coronavirus, which lowered global CO_2 emissions to 25 billion metric tons. The prize is a sailboat cruise.

JUNE 2, 2104. Viking *Miami* turned away. The 12,500-nautical-acre cruise city refused entry to Reykjavík after asylum seekers flood Glasgow and Lerwick.

JUNE 16, 2263. First woman in space. Clarke Station hosts tricentennial concert celebrating Valentina Tereshkova, whose *Vostok 6* orbited Earth 48 times in 1963.

JUNE 19, 2089. Alphabet sells Wayless, a one-way time transporter for liquids only, to Diageo-Chivas for undisclosed Bitcoin sum. Single malt prices poised to surge.

JUNE 24, 2029. Cat-o'-nine-tails. Massachusetts National Guard reintroduces flogging for unwanted sexual advances and smoking. Medically supervised.

JULY 4, 2029. Reverse lottery. Interim POTUS orders treasury sec to draw one billionaire's name a month for total confiscation in return for health and auto care. "Fair enough," says Bezos.

JULY 14, 2122. Semper Fi. Repurposed US Marine Corps delivers CAEVID-55 vaccine worldwide in 14 days, winning Nobel Peace Patch, suitable for hat or sleeve.

JULY 19, 2045. UFO farewell. Indiana hobbyist Paul Hoachs, whose tiny saucer-size drones astonished the faithful for over 90 years, dies at 101. Small things are often mistaken for large things farther away.

JULY 29, 2024. Genre for $400. Rudy Rucker, first American science fiction author to be a *Jeopardy* answer, is awarded six tickets to the summer SFWA distance dance.

AUGUST 7, 2105. Unicide gun. Johnson & Johnson's snakeshot pistol, which only fires when gripped by adult owner's teeth, is endorsed by AARP: "Leaves no mess for loved ones!"

AUGUST 11, 2077. Reparations. RepCom awards descendants of slaves lifetime health care with dental. Cash awards for lynching, segregation and redlining still in committee.

AUGUST 19, 2055. Whoopi Goldberg passes. The beloved former veep (under Biden) ceases texting at age 99. Away is where she passed to.

AUGUST 27, 2028. Space Force Academy dedication. Cadets launch hats as POTUS cuts ribbon on Cape Kennedy campus. Two-year program to include FTL science, zodiacal psych and conversational Vulcan.

SEPTEMBER 1, 2026. SS *presente*! Interim POTUS Andrew Yang adds 13-person Sudden Solutions team to emergency cabinet. Silent Majority streams screams of protest.

SEPTEMBER 4, 2026. New$chool year begins. HEW to pay public high school students $150 per week with $1,500 graduation bonus. "Education = collaboration" tweets SS chair Cortez.

SEPTEMBER 11, 2026. Home run. Mass incarceration ends at 9:15 a.m. EST, with 99.44% of US prison population met at open gates by families, friends, community volunteers. Bells toll coast to coast.

SEPTEMBER 12, 2120. Centennial salute. WHO declares Lake of the Ozarks a COVID-19 World Heritage Site.

OCTOBER 4, 2028. Unlike Ike. Eisenhower portrait removed from Kansas statehouse. The two-term US president smoked 3 to 4 packs a day during World War II. D-Day no exception.

OCTOBER 12, 2116. Hands off. Venus rover *Romeo* finds uninhabited city near Planitia Llorona. SpaceX protocol bans "contact without explicit invite." Still waiting.

OCTOBER 20, 2154. Last call? Cannibal Club, the legendary secret eatery where Hollywood stars dine on human flesh, said to close. QAcademy's "no comment," Truth's triumphant nod.

OCTOBER 25, 2066. Confiscatory? IRS insists that new 99% wealth tax applies only to those millions that were made with help of highways, public education, Internet or US Treasury services. All other millions tax exempt.

NOVEMBER 2, 2066. Crack-up. A 5-degree-wide black band appears to bisect the Milky Way as seen from Earth. The entire galaxy is apparently gone before the lunar month ends.

NOVEMBER 14, 2077. Unlethal award. The genetically dehanced murder hornet bioengineered by All Blue Entertainment is awarded a Tech Emmy in Crowd Control.

NOVEMBER 22, 2206. Finally! Eurocon's Earth rover *Nemo* surfaces in Aegean Sea after mapping the unseen 71% of the planet's 510 trillion square meters for the first time. Nobody notices.

NOVEMBER 24, 2111. Delete all. Brazil joins Hungary in prohibiting written language. Literacy, once widely admired, is denounced by many since The Downheaval as a seditious waste of time.

DECEMBER 3, 2208. Sold! Wuhan buys Venice, second European city to be reconstituted on Yangtse River. CCP's 3D replicator to duplicate itself upon completion of Shanghai's Budapest. Originals to be destroyed.

DECEMBER 15, 2099. Trueky™ triumph. Hopper ranchers hurl hats in air and crawler feedlots flinch as drumsticks reach $77 per pound on Chicago Insect Xchange, topping reelbeaf™ patties for first time.

DECEMBER 19, 2104. Monsters overrun North Atlanta suburbs. Diminutive but deadly, Georgia Tech's research simulmice were DNAed with a fierce need for escape and revenge. The name was originally a joke.

DECEMBER 25, 2208. Christmas duel. India's Krishna minerbot is challenged by Iceland's Troll, on Eumonia, the largest of the inner asteroids. AI honor code is law in tinyplanet claim disputes.

2021

JANUARY 2, 2188. Farewell. Feral pigs inherit Houston, first American city to be off-lawed entire as wet-bulb temp hits 35°C. Climate Emergency Protocols allow no return even to bourn the dead.

JANUARY 12, 2102. Toothbrush of the stars. Sotheby's sets auction floor of $2.5 million. First owned by Cary Grant, later by Lady Gaga and Steph Curry, the Colgate 360 is being sold by Curry's great-granddaughter, Esso.

JANUARY 17, 2076. Next exit. Prompted by a Nebraska ammonium truck spill and an unseasonable rain, Interstate 80's self-sealing biosurface veers NW at 1.4 mph. Canada's Tar Sands thought to be goal.

JANUARY 22, 2028. Enroll today! Reconfigured as a no-residency online civics academy, the Electoral College awards the diploma required to vote in presidential elections. Tuition-free to US residents.

FEBRUARY 1, 2067. Blockchain bites! Crude oil prices tank with release of rescoins set to rise 8% in value every year that fossil fuels remain in the ground. Venezuela, Canada rush to buy in.

FEBRUARY 16, 2215. Longitudinal study. Defying inner planet protocols, Indonesian probe seeds Venus with microbial soil to see if vertebrate life will emerge.

FEBRUARY 22, 2026. Merica first. Red Hat Militia seizes Kenosha, Wisconsin, as FoxFlicks livestreams. Tactical Colonel Snapp denies "coupe" [*sic*], promises election "when originals attain."

FEBRUARY 29, 2021. Twofer. Library of Congress declares February 29 Science Fiction Writers Day. Every fourth February 29 will honor America's Fortune Cookie Writers.

MARCH 3, 2225. Dangerous when wet. Bicentennial of the death of "Sunny" Carl, accidental discoverer of Sun Paint, which both captures and stores solar energy. A Maaco touch-up artist, Carl died mixing the color that saved the world.

MARCH 10, 2026. Past due. POTUS Chang signs new IRS bill taxing churches at full corporate rate, plus the 12.5% "landslide" penalty imposed on enterprises trafficking in "false or baseless claims."

MARCH 27, 2108. High-end cruise. Holland-America welcomes first 110 guests to refurbished International Space Station. The

ISS *Clarke* features 125 staterooms, period gym and a zero-G waterless pool with a kiddie section.

MARCH 29, 2055. Gypsy pass. All migrants and refugees awarded world xitizenship by UNICEF. Rights include open borders everywhere, plus ⅗ access to all educational, medical and housing benefits.

APRIL 1, 2308. Oumuamua's back! The alien spaceship first sighted in 2017 returns to park in Earth polar orbit. According to SETI diplomats, it's here to say aloha. But that's all we know so far.

APRIL 6, 2034. NASCAR buys Stonehenge. Sold by Charles to compensate Ulster deportees, it will appear in the Talladega infield alongside 1,165 Confederate memorials and three statues of Donald J. Trump, one unfinished.

APRIL 18, 2103. Nobel sword dance. Some 350 Russians in bright green *ushanka*s—flaps up for spring—perform in Red Square to honor New Soviet Union's Azov-Kolskaya Rotary, the prize-winning jet stream wind farm.

APRIL 24, 2071. Call of the wild. Cities and suburbs worldwide panic as 114 labs and collies kill their owners or walkers, the most fatalities in one day since urban coyotes began to sniff and bond with leashed pets in 2066.

MAY 7, 2054. MayDay Week. Vietnam joins with Cuba, Soviet Union II, Bolivaran Union and China in full dress parade celebrating centennial of Điện Biên Phủ, the first military defeat of colonialism.

MAY 7, 2106. Shook up. Leaning Tower of Pisa straightens as RS 4.4 quake rattles Tuscany. No other casualties.

MAY 9, 2033. Reparations. Honoring birthday of John Brown, President Abrams signs 40 Acres Act, then gifts the pen to Henry Louis Gates Jr., chair of Black Ancestry Fund, charged with retiring the debt.

MAY 24, 2112. Long gone. Last snow patch on Everest disappears. The last snow on Kilimanjaro disappeared on May 24, 2031. Noting synchronicity, Dalai Lama weeps for both, and for us all.

JUNE 2, 2028. Proud girls. Gender-equal Congress overrides President Yang's angry veto of AOC's "No-Billions" bill. Yeas all awarded pink CONFISCATORY? PROUDLY SO! pens by Majority Leader Warren.

JUNE 12, 2125. *AI v. AI*. Tortbuster, the first AI to pass the California bar exam, represents Writers Guild in efforts to deny membership to Oscar-nominee Genrewriter.

JUNE 16, 2054. Depistoled. LAPD and 17,922 other police departments disarmed under Reparations Protocols, which require all armed peace officers to be graduates of Social Service Academy in Denver.

JUNE 21, 2216. En garde! Security drone embedded in Saturn's rings. It is hoped that SPATO's deadly *Galileo* will ward off Taliban suicide drones trying to "erase" the "unclean" Anthe ring.

JULY 4, 2027. Dog talk. Petco sales soar with new 16-word bark replacer. Vocab, selected by head angle, includes "poopout," "love you" and "food time." Voice by Frances McDormand.

JULY 11, 2049. Future tents. Conselo, the WHO refugee camp, hits 50 million, surpassing Delhi as world's largest city. It is steadily growing from Turkey into what was once Bulgaria.

JULY 16, 2104. Green zeps. Citing climate concerns, Southwest replaces its retiring jet fleet with short-haul electric airships. The 400,000 max-clean routes are expected to reduce US emissions by one-third.

JULY 30, 2055. No returns. Amazon offers space burial, which includes launch into 30-day (approx.) unstable orbit, with "glorious" cremation on atmospheric reentry.

AUGUST 3, 2105. Atacama Giant hoax. The 119-meter geoglyph "discovered" on Mars as evidence of transplanetary ancients is revealed to be a Chilean fake. Chinese rover to erase.

AUGUST 13, 2114. Three bells. Global sea level rise, record Bitcoin low and teen suicides intersect at 1.6 M/$/K, securing a third trifecta for the long-misunderstood science of numerology.

AUGUST 19, 2206. Partial cattle. World Wellness Nobel nod goes to Rollos™, the paddle-legged, rumenfree feedlot stock developed by KizerGen. Climate heroes, they are largely eyeless.

AUGUST 26, 2059. Sudden stop! All 4,023,360 kilometers of US fossil fuel pipelines disabled by ecoware cybermilitia Gretazons. Klicks replaced miles when the USA went metric on July 4, 2056.

SEPTEMBER 5, 2065. Death penalty dies. Supreme Court, in a 9–6 vote, rules decades on death row "cruel and unusual," and so unconstitutional. National lottery to select one to be publicly hanged—and the remaining 3,914 set free.

SEPTEMBER 9, 2308. Oumuamua arrival. After four silent months in polar Earth orbit, the comet-like interstellar ship suddenly descends into Barents Sea. Still no word. Russian Coast Guard to investigate.

SEPTEMBER 16, 2120. *Days of Then* disaster. The popular Vegas variety show, featuring randomized gunfire for those who aspire to be survivors of mass shootings, closes down when all 1,566 survive and sue for full refunds plus damages.

SEPTEMBER 26, 2077. Sea snot rescue. RefugeeRelief™ agrees to remove, bale and distribute the white marine mucilage which covers the Aegean Sea. The tasteless algae is entirely edible, but only by the very poor.

OCTOBER 3, 2055. Manatees occupy assisted living facility. Crystal River Elder Care evacuated without injuries. The aquatic mammals have evolved to leave the water for hours or even days, seeking cable TV.

OCTOBER 12, 2103. Oval Office mishap. Carmine Olman Indigo torn apart by gorilla. This is the first time, ever, that a sitting US president has been killed by an endangered species.

OCTOBER 20, 2044. Guantananomo. Using their new powers, WHO commandos airlift 40 Guantanamo detainees to Havana resort, citing health risk of indefinite confinement. Pentagon to drop appeal.

OCTOBER 31, 2128. Trick or treat. Indonesian rover seeks asylum at Musk Moon Hotel. First asylum appeal by a robot, one of 111 now roaming the lunar surface. The US Space Force maintains a suite at the hotel.

NOVEMBER 3, 2066. All aboard! Everest summit declared World Heritage Site. China's North Ridge Funicular will operate year-round, making the attraction accessible to all. Sierra Club praises Chinese Communist Party.

NOVEMBER 14, 2267. Heat dome. Nashville, Tennessee, sets new US record: 100 consecutive days over 140°F (60°C). People used to live here.

NOVEMBER 16, 2099. Ghost control. POTUS Cortez bans ghost (or LEGO) guns nationwide unless assembled in Texas or Kentucky for affairs of honor. NRA expected to appeal.

NOVEMBER 16, 2115. Scandinavian virus. WHO announces that the optical corona variant that has blinded one-third of the world's population originated in the aurora borealis. Iceland to apologize.

DECEMBER 2, 2119. Full moon. First sequence test of NASA's lunar asteroid attractor is blamed for monster tide that made Bahamas disappear overnight. No sign of survivors.

DECEMBER 15, 2066. Grounded. Using its new powers, WHO adds $500 carbon fee to every commercial flight, regardless of distance or duration. Expected to reduce air travel 91%, improve atmospheric health 6%.

DECEMBER 19, 2204. Flop! Cable failure drops jet stream wind farm into North Sea. No casualties, but Euro-wide blackout threatens Xmas!

DECEMBER 22, 2145. Mushrooms over Africa. Atomic bombs flatten both Lagos and Nairobi as proxy war escalates to nuclear weapons; first use since 1945. Chinese Communist Party to sanction both ISIS and Israel.

2022

JANUARY 1, 2067. DOA? CDC awards every US citizen over 65 who accepts a DNR tattoo a $65,000 annual bonus. Also available to newborns and all certified homeless.

JANUARY 9, 2088. Good greef! GMO coral blocks Panama Canal. The mobile hybrid, designed to seek and replace dying Caribbean reefs, is instead drawn to concrete. Monsanto promises a fix.

JANUARY 14, 2035. Touchdown! LDS temple lands on moon. The one-way spaceship will be visible worldwide with special glasses. Blue Origin founder Bezos is a recent convert to the 19th-century religion.

JANUARY 22, 2105. Restricted speech. Originalist SCOTUS rules that corporations are not "free persons" but ⅗ only. Can speak but not publish, vote, lobby or marry.

FEBRUARY 9, 2104. Cripz™ elected mayor of Chicago, now the 11th (and largest) American city to be ruled by a constitutionalized gang. Defeated Proud Boyz™ demand recount.

FEBRUARY 12, 2042. One hundred candles. Teresa Bloom, Blue Origin's celebrated first centenarian in space, chokes on birthday cake during zero-G ceremony. Bezos maneuver unsuccessful.

FEBRUARY 14, 2214. Look out. Alarming astronomers, Jupiter's Great Red Spot lifts off the giant planet. Once thought to be a storm, the device is apparently headed for the inner planets, of which Earth is one.

FEBRUARY 21, 2084. Treaty win. Mount Rushmore, three-diminued for removal, is relocated to Alcatraz Island, where it will be displayed along with Confederate, Custer, Trump and other memorials one day each year.

MARCH 6, 2111. Drone work. Patton Peace Prize awarded to Israel, which invaded, conquered and occupied Lebanon last year with zero military casualties; collaterals only, and damn few of them.

MARCH 11, 2029. Altruism in action. Militant vaccine refusal is single symptom of new COVID variant, which CDC names "Altrucon," as it exists only to provide ample friendly hosts for other infections.

MARCH 19, 2133. Anon for now. Earth's 122 largest refugee camps awarded single UN Security Council seat. New nation of 266 million needs only a name to provide passports, anthem and constitution. Amazon offers pro bono help.

MARCH 23, 2077. Game of chance. Indianapolis high school Suicide Club suspended after members sold lottery tickets to hire an assassin for "sudden, unexpected death without trauma." Lotteries are illegal for minors in several states.

APRIL 1, 2132. Provo jab. Johnson&™ patents vaccine for virus that does not yet exist. US Patent Office stipulates that new variant must be developed within one year.

APRIL 11, 2074. Go green! Using a long-forgotten power to fight global warming, Congress limits Pentagon operations and personnel to US territory absent a formal (written) declaration of war.

APRIL 18, 2111. Tradin' paint. VW, Kia and Ford entries wipe out in NASCAR's Le Moont lunar rover race. With the field reduced to two, Tesla's wry Ricky Bobby calls his win over Toyota a "one-checker flag."

APRIL 22, 2056. Right to life. Texas awards new fetal citizens $1,750 monthly remittance to house and feed their female hosts. Remittance withdrawn with Texans' first breath.

MAY 1, 2058. Last call. A global cyberhack floods cell phones worldwide with mayday calls, as if climate change were a crash about to happen. Which it is. IPCC extends "No comment" from its secret Thunberg retreat.

MAY 3, 2106. Last best friend. RIP Fetch, 9, dead of undisclosed injuries in a Newark EVR. Dogs have been in a steep decline since 2155, when a bat-rat hybrid (brat) being developed as a self-cloning novelty pet escaped from a Purina lab. Brats prey on dogs for fun.

MAY 11, 2024. Undictment. In a discretionary order, Supreme Court dismisses Trump's criminal indictments, ruling that all efforts by a defeated president to overturn his defeat are constitutionally protected self-defense.

MAY 23, 2213. Bull's-eye. On its third pass through our solar system, Oumuamua penetrates and ignites the gas giant Jupiter, now a dim dwarf star orbiting Sol. Mission accomplished?

JUNE 7, 2255. Suez Canal closes. The famed sea-level passage from east to west operated for 386 years, declining with the advent of jet stream sail transport. The final decades saw only yachts and kayakers.

JUNE 20, 2104. Spaniels knighted. Some 2.4 million clones of Squire Paws, the royal favorite of Charles III, the last British monarch, are awarded the OBE. Identical and affectionate, they answer only to "Sir."

JUNE 24, 2028. Fake news? US Election Commission removes the twice-defeated deceased ex-president from the 2028 ballot. His TruthSocial™ tweets insist that he is still alive, though he has not been seen in person since 2026.

JUNE 31, 2042. *Lunar Princess* vanishes. Blue Origin's first cruise ship to orbit the moon loses visual and radio contact on passing to the dark side. The ship and its 144 passengers and crew are never seen again.

JULY 5, 2155. Aloha, South Pacific Gyre! In its boldest move since independence, Hawaii annexes the profitable, plastic-rich Great Pacific Garbage Patch. The colorful, bouncy surface attracts both kayakers and jellowars, staple seafood of the homeless.

JULY 11, 2029. Médecins Sans Frontières opens 12 US clinics. The acclaimed international MDs will provide reproductive health care, including abortion, to underserved Americans.

JULY 18, 2111. Sandstorm swallows Timbuktu. North Africa's best (and only) tourist attraction since the controlled demolition of the Pyramids of Giza is not expected to reappear. Year-old storm still rages.

JULY 24, 2089. Iran and Pakistan schedule eight-day war. The conflict, to be fought in Lebanon's Bekaa Valley by Kurdish mercenaries, is to settle a maintenance issue aboard the International Space Mosque. No date set.

AUGUST 6, 2055. In its first ruling since okaying its own "veiled expansion," the US Supreme Court finds the Constitution itself unconstitutional, "but only just." The veil obscures number, gender, party, tenure and names of justices. Host ship lands on moon.

AUGUST 11, 2104. Crisis in Mecca. Cardiac transplant recipients with organic vat-grown hearts banned from Hajj as swine stem cells can be found in transplants. Blasphemy in Islam can carry the death penalty; in Judaism, a wry shrug.

AUGUST 18, 2024. Drone swarm runs off 500,000 pro-abortion demonstrators in DC. The bee-size electricals are "harmless to humans," assures Homeland Security, "but fatal to murderous mobs. Plus, demanding things contrary to settled law is obviously unlawful."

AUGUST 28, 2287. AI church? Twelve Mars rovers converge around a crude shrine of blue stones, bump together, then dismantle and bury one of their own: a form of worship, some say, generated by AI, since blue stones and sacrifice alike are unknown on Mars.

SEPTEMBER 2, 2023. Exactly 100 years after the first free elections in independent Ireland, Prop32 passes in Northern Ireland, freeing the "six counties" to join Éire and quit Great Britain.

SEPTEMBER 13, 2071. CDC closes law schools and comedy clubs to slow spread of COVID variant Y-16, which reshapes the larynx and is transmitted by words of seven syllables or clever questions.

SEPTEMBER 21, 2102. Gibraltar's overcrowded Caravan Bridge collapses. Estimated 110,117 die in the worst tragedy since the WHO's Émigré Act gave refugees the right to go anywhere but stay nowhere.

SEPTEMBER 28, 2311. The hole in the universe first spotted by NASA's Webbscope in 2022 has doubled in size and appears to be headed toward our galaxy. US Space Force astrologers counsel courage, calm, alarm.

OCTOBER 6, 2075. Making it real. Inspired by new state license tag calling California Ohlone Land, Governor Laughing Bear levies a 2.7% fee on all California real estate transactions, to be shared by Native tribes and groups.

OCTOBER 11, 2215. In a historic first, Station Ivy, the orbital resort–lounge for Ivy League alumni, votes to admit "acceptable" grads of Grinnell, a small midwestern college. Princeton, Yale threaten boycott.

OCTOBER 22, 2108. No no nukes. Using its new powers, WHO bans and dismantles all nuclear weapons. Almost. Holdouts Israel, United States and Pakistan penalized with six-month sovereignty dehancement.

OCTOBER 30, 2031. Trick or treat. Children (ages 3–16) of all nations awarded seat on UN Security Council. Their masked regent is Greta Thernburg, 28, former director of the UN's Ministry for the Future.

NOVEMBER 5, 2103. Senate confirms Tortmaster™ to US Supreme Court. Raytheon's judicial AI, now the 19th Justice and first fully artificial one, will also assist Deputy Vice President Kirkland in counting electoral votes.

NOVEMBER 14, 2030. Prince Andrew, Duke of York, the first British royal family member to leave planet Earth, rides SpaceX *Falcon* to the International Space Station. He is not expected to return.

NOVEMBER 21, 2087. Murder hornet kit found in Saudi diplomat's United carry-on. Waiving diplomatic immunity, he was rebooked on Emirates. Murder hornets are not permitted on mixed-gender flights, even in kit form.

NOVEMBER ?, 2216. Paulo "Loco" Fogo, the Brazilian indigene activist whose mad cow pandemicator saved the Amazon and wiped out the global beef industry, dies in Guantanamo IX at 99. Exact date and manner of death withheld.

DECEMBER 5, 2121. Remnants of Amadora (NEA 44821), demolished (instead of deflected) by Asteroid Alert, obliterate pyramids, most of Holland, San Francisco Bay Bridge and 1.6 million people. Earth will pass through debris cloud again in late 2125.

DECEMBER 8, 2159. Mount Scranton erupts for first time as tourists applaud. The 2,909-meter volcano, formed by a vibratory fracking incident in 2111, is the highest mountain east of the Mississippi, and the only one still growing.

DECEMBER 18, 2035. Cloud cleans up Internet. An apparently self-created AI calling itself "Clauwde" [*sic*] deletes, then wipes

Twitter and TikTok and promises more to follow. Wikipedia ponders possible appeals.

DECEMBER 24, 2024. In a surprise move, Haitian gangs stand down and join millions in airport sit-ins as Aristide's exiled Lavalas government declares the country off-limits to international "peacekeepers." So far, so good.

2023

JANUARY 2, 2049. Convention of States (39) ratifies Great Amenditure [*sic*] of US Constitution in secret ballot. Site of convention, names of states and new clauses withheld (nondisclosure clause #4).

JANUARY 7, 2216. Tenth planet, Dix, joins solar system. The deep-space body, which entered the heliosphere at .09c, is captured by Sol in an eccentric orbit "still to be discovered," according to Société Planétaire.

JANUARY 11, 2071. Dogs outnumber people in first pet census of USA: 410 million vs. 394 million. Homeless humans still outnumber stray dogs 3 to 1.6. Asked her response to census, President Cleigh hugs her corgi, Potus.

JANUARY 23, 2106. Cuba votes to lift sanctions on USA. The New World Soviet, representing the Caribbean nations, Mexico and Canada, votes Aye to reward "even baby steps against climate crisis."

FEBRUARY 3, 2081. Olympic Committee adds pinball. Athletes, representing 11 nations, will all compete on a single five-ball, two-flipper machine, developed in secret by Bally and introduced day of competition.

FEBRUARY 14, 2206. Venus's new ring makes its first appearance at dusk on Valentine's Day. Assembled from comet ice debris by Space XV and Hallmarque, it is projected to last "longer than most marriages."

FEBRUARY 16, 2031. US Supreme Court okays House Ways and Means Committee Patriots. The 6–3 vote rules militias constitutional if well regulated and properly armed. Uniforms suggested but not required.

FEBRUARY 25, 2122. Ukraine War centennial. International honor guard salutes the conflict for its contributions to public discipline, drone diplomacy, collateral sacrifice—and as an "ongoing memorial to war itself." All hats off!

MARCH 9, 2036. International Cartographers Association charts the Ariel River, Earth's first permanent (and mappable) atmospheric river. From the warming subarctic, the Ariel flows 4,250 kilometers to its wide, dark mouth on the California coast, where the cities of Salinas and Monterey used to be.

MARCH 17, 2177. Meri wins Gramaphone Award for *Dreeems*, their symphony that puts audiences immediately to sleep. After 39 minutes, all awaken refreshed, with a warm regard for others that can last for two to three days.

MARCH 24, 2116. Facebook seeks admission to UN. The part-time population of 1.2 billion, world's third largest, gets along under loosely libertarian bureaucratic rule. What's not to Like?

MARCH 27, 2088. US Constitution Amendment 77 ratified! It makes racial discrimination constitutional, even mandatory, when in accord with the Reparations Amendment (the 76th). Ivy League alumni gather to complain.

APRIL 1, 2029. Trillion-dollar pewter coin minted for US Federal Reserve. Heads depicts President AOC arriving and tails, Trump departing. It can be found in a secret vault somewhere.

APRIL 12, 2061. First baby born in space. A 23-inch boy, Yurivitch, weight yet unknown, is delivered by C-section aboard the International Space Station during centennial toast to the first human in space. *Na zdorovie!*

APRIL 22, 2091. Cheers and boats rise together as the Columbia pipeline connecting The Dalles, Oregon, with Lake Mead, Nevada, is opened in a last attempt to restore the Colorado River and the city of Las Vegas.

APRIL 29, 2108. WHO and UN both recognize world's first tricity state. Singapore, Hong Kong and Guam to share sovereignty, citizenship and mutual defense. United States and China to object. Louis Vuitton to design flag.

MAY 4, 2077. US Supreme Court returns West Virginia to Virginia as reparation for Civil War losses and grants statehood to Taiwan in accordance with its ruling that the flag can never again be altered.

MAY 12, 2104. Cardinals assemble in the Vatican to view and mourn the first female pontiff, Pope Sister Mary, killed in the crash of United 292. Hers is the first human body to be created with a 3D printer.

MAY 21, 2101. Wagner Group buys West Point. Graduates of the six-month program will receive a uniform with epaulets and a deployment in the mercenary service, which is proudly serving on both sides of the long-running Russia-Ukraine conflict.

MAY 22, 2076. Singin' in the rain. A cisgender couple in Burberrys is married in Halifax, Nova Scotia, "because of rather than despite" the yearlong rain which has emptied the city. They then dance.

JUNE 7, 2111. Shanghai joins LA and Tokyo with lectro-only laws. Seattle and Seoul still holding out. The hybrid spaniels, which excrete no solid waste, still must be walked and fed daily. London claims to be waiting for "full electrics."

JUNE 13, 2029. Oumuamua, the interstellar object that sped through our solar system in 2017, returns—and after one Earth orbit, departs again. "We are not alone," says Harvard scientist Avi Loeb. "As important a discovery as Galileo's that our Earth is not the center of the universe."

JUNE 17, 2107. Taiwan bans waving cats (*maneko neki*) as spy devices for the mainland Communist government. The welcoming Chinese restaurant figures are said to secretly measure popular attitudes to annexation.

JUNE 27, 2314. Half-Earth. E. O. Wilson's dream (and prescription) is achieved with the removal of humans from Europe's Białowieża Forest. The 51% is celebrated as not the end but the flowering of the Anthropocene.

JULY 4, 2029. Happy birthday. POTUS AOC signs Federal Misinformation Limitation Act to muted applause. All US currency is to be replaced, with the falsehood "In God We Trust" removed.

JULY 11–15, 2055. Tourists flee as Great Atlantic Sargassam Belt lands on Florida coast. Heinz claims cleanup rights as the smelly brown seaweed is a key ingredient in their all-plant fish sticks, Possible™.

JULY 16, 2107. For the first time, shredding tops both burial and cremation in American funeral popularity. Green New Dealers claim climate victory, while undertakers and morticians continue to complain of the shrill sound.

JULY 23, 2143. As Amazon and Windsor delivery drones battle over Liverpool and London, Queen Betty III pleas for RAF intervention in Second Battle of Britain and promises royal discounts.